THE ANGELA TANNER FILES

BOOKS 1 & 2

C.D. GORRI

CASTING MAGIC

THE REALITY MAY CHANGE EVERYTHING.

Things in Northern New Jersey just got a little more intense for Angela Tanner. She is a Witch who hasn't come into her powers yet, but things go full speed ahead when her father is accused of a crime he didn't commit.

Enter Jody Nieves. The tall, dark, and powerful Guardian is sent to fetch her and observe as she tries to clear her father's name. He does more than that, he wakes up a part of her she never dreamed existed.

Can she save her father in time, trust that Jody's attentions are genuine, and discover the truth about her own powers?

Find out in this first installment of the Angela Tanner Files.

CASTING MAGIC

THE ANGELA TANNER FILES
VOLUME I

The smile on my face left as we turned the corner away from the holiday festivities of the DiPaolo-Kelly home. I love Thanksgiving. It was such a warm and homey holiday. Well, for other people it was. As my driver accelerated the car my stomach twisted itself in knots. I really didn't want to go home. What was the point? No one would be there anyway.

I brushed a hand over my head in a vain attempt to control my overzealous curls, but they just weren't havin' any of that. My hair had a mind of its own. I used to wear it long and pulled back in a super tight, thick braid *every single day* of grade school.

That was my mom's rule. She was a little strict about appearance. But once I entered high school, I had a revelation. *My head, my hair, my rules.* I went to a salon that was owned by a close friend of the family and had her chop it off. Every year I did the same thing, right before school started in September, I cut it just above my shoulders.

Of course when Sherry styled it, it looked awesome! On days when *I* tried to style my hair, it sort of just curled all over the place. I usually threw on a wide headband to keep it out of my face, especially in school. I'm a junior this year. I go to Sacred Heart Preparatory School in Northern, New Jersey. It's a Catholic high school, but it's co-ed, thank the goddess!

Oh yeah, I'm a Witch. I come from a long line of Witches. We are called the Coven Realta. Loosely translated it means Coven of Light or Starlight. We are small and we follow both Wiccan and Asatru practices, though a lot of what we do is not public knowledge. I am not sure of my powers yet, I'm still young and not everyone has a *talent* or *gift* for magic.

Lately, I've been more and more afraid that I might fall into that category. The *unmagicked* in our Coven are treated the same as everyone. I'm lucky in that aspect. I've heard of Covens who banish their *unmagicked* or worse, kill them. But those are just stories, I think.

Anyway, we of the Coven Realta are supposed to

be in touch with the natural rhythm of the life cycles of all living things, plant animal and mineral. Nurturers, gardeners, healers, that type of thing. But not me. I've always been more comfortable behind a keyboard than at the other end of a shovel or rake.

I've been trying to figure out just what I am good at these past few months with help of course. You see, Sherry isn't just my stylist, she is my mentor. She used my Dad's firm a few years back to help out with some legal documents. She came to our house once to sign papers when I was about eight. That's when we first met. She took me under her wing, and I was forever grateful.

My father is a very successful businessman. What it is that he does exactly, I am not really sure. His firm dabbles in law, accounting, real estate, public relations, and just about everything there is. His company is called Tanner Global Enterprises, or TGE for short. He has offices in a huge high rise in Manhattan. I don't get to see him very much, but we have a good relationship.

I know he is a gifted Witch and I am really hoping that I take after him. We have a huge orchard of apple and pear trees behind our home that he tends. His success in business is directly related to those trees. The way I understand it is this, a healthy orchard for my father, means a healthy company. Cool, right?

Anyway, whatever relationship I have with my Dad, it is the total opposite with my mom. She is not very gifted in magic. I was seven the first time I understood that she used flirtation and desire to get what she wanted. I thought she must be so powerful to get so many people to treat her like a princess, but as I got older, I understood it a little better. She never seems to enjoy our Solstice gatherings or any of our Coven's celebrations. She is sort of vain and silly, I guess. All I know is I never seem to please her.

She is tall and thin, willowy, I guess. She has lovely straight blonde hair, big blue eyes and a pouty mouth. She looks like a supermodel. I look *nothing* like her. My father isn't so bad either. He is also tall and thin, with jet black hair and dark eyes. He's really handsome, but more importantly he is sweet and loving. Mom, not so much.

I don't know who I look like. Maybe some forgotten aunt or uncle? *Oh, well.* After the fiasco that was my six-week stint at fat camp the past summer I have learned to accept myself for who I am. I am 5'5" tall (or short depending on my mood), I weigh 145 pounds, and you got it, I am a ginger. A serious one.

My hair is bright red, not auburn or mahogany, I

am talking bright, orangey red. It is super curly and, you guessed it, it gets super frizzy in the rain. My skin is very pale, and I have a splattering of freckles over my nose and shoulders though they have gotten a lot lighter since I was a kid. The ones on my face are hardly visible especially after I put on some make-up.

I do have pretty nice eyes. They are hazel, not quite blue but not quite green, and I swear I once saw them turn violet when I was angry at my mom. That's good news for a Witch. That usually meant a Witch's powers were coming. I can't wait for mine. Maybe then Mom will be proud of me. But even if she isn't, it will still be cool.

Anyway, my mind drifted back to the small party I had just left. My best friend Grazi looked like she had just been through something rough. I could tell she wanted to talk, but we had secrets between us. She didn't know I was a Witch and I didn't tell her I knew she was a Werewolf.

Still, it was nice to pretend for a little while that I was just a normal kid celebrating the holidays. When I got into the car Daddy had hired to drive me around, I almost forgot for a moment that I would be going back to a big empty house. It was Thanksgiving, Daddy had to work, and Mom was never big on the holidays. That's one reason why I went to celebrate with Grazi.

Her grandmother made a truly incredible meal. I never tasted home cooked food like that before. My parents rarely eat with me and when they do, we are at a restaurant. During the week I usually just order take out. I've tried my hand at cooking before. It was so not my thing. I truly suck at it.

Anyway, we sang happy birthday, ate a delicious cake made entirely out of cream puffs, and afterwards we even played board games, like a real family. I didn't want it to end, but Grazi looked beat. I could tell by the vibes she was giving off that she was in pain and needed to heal. I gave her a gentle hug before I left. I really wanted to tell her the truth already. I just had to figure out how.

You see Werewolves, especially Hounds of God, tended to be tight asses. They followed a crap load of rules and didn't like outsiders. American Packs sometimes worked with white Witches, but European Packs had a hard time with all Witches. Especially the Hounds, who worked for the Catholic Church. They tended to group all Witches together in one clump as evil. Talk about unfair! *Hmph.*

So I was sitting in the backseat of the Lincoln Town Car and was enjoying the cream puff Nonna had insisted I take home with me when the car swerved dramatically to the right. I dropped my iPhone, cream puff, and bottled water and held on for all I was worth. When we came to a stop it was sudden and hard. My seatbelt pulled tight around my stomach and thighs. That was definitely going to leave bruise! What the heck did we hit? A bull?

I was breathing hard and scared as heck and that was before the door closest to me was ripped off its hinges by a force so powerful it melted the remaining metal. I gasped and struggled to get the seatbelt off when a figure appeared right in front of me. I couldn't tell what it was. The seatbelt wouldn't budge! The figure was dark and misshapen with hollow sockets instead of eyes. I opened my mouth and did the only thing an almost seventeen-year-old Witch could do. I closed my eyes and screamed.

The thing reached a clawed hand towards me then a second later he was lifted and thrown through the air. He screeched unintelligibly and landed with a thud a few feet from the car. That's when I saw *him*. He had long hair for a guy. It reached the top of his shoulders. It was dark and curly and looked perfect against the olive toned complexion of his skin. He wore a black leather coat, tight pants, and black combat boots.

He turned to face the thing that had ripped off my door. They moved out of my line of vision and I renewed my struggle against the seatbelt. The car was pushed up against the guardrail of Changebridge Road, which incidentally was just ten minutes away from my house. I wished I could get out of the car and run, but I couldn't budge. I heard a zap and a thud, they were fighting! An honest to goddess battle right in front of me and I was missing half of it.

The creature landed with a crash a few feet in front of me and I watched in horror as he removed the offending weapon from his rib cage and stood up as if nothing had happened. The dark stranger adjusted his stance and removed a large and wicked looking knife from his boot. It was an Athame. The black handle disappeared in his hand, but the blade shone bright in the moonlight. It was marked with several symbols, wards and protection spells for its bearer. It was a beautiful piece.

For a second, I felt like I was in *WolfMoon,* the online game for supernatural beings that I had been playing for years. Normals played it too, they just didn't realize things like Witches, Demons, Werewolves, Goblins, Vampires, Fairies and Trolls were real. I couldn't really understand why they thought we were all fake, I mean did they honestly imagine regular people could dream this stuff up? *Pllleeease.*

"Watch out!" I yelled as the thing charged, teeth bared, and claws extended. It seemed to radiate heat from its insides. The place where it had been hit oozed a lava-like blood that hissed and melted the snow on the ground as soon as it hit.

The stranger in black lifted his left hand and muttered a string of phrases, but I was too far away to make them out. Cold white light spurted from his hand and the eyeless figure stopped in his tracks. He started to spurt and shake and right before my eyes he vanished in a cloud of dark smoke and ash. I had never seen anything like it. That type of weaponized magic was unknown to me. Sherry and my Dad were businesspeople, not warriors. It was scary and beautiful to watch. I was intrigued in spite of my natural instinct to get the heck out of there.

The darkness on the road was broken only by the headlights of the town car. It was so cold I could see my breath. But the cold didn't seem to affect the dude who just vanquished the thing that tried to attack me. My life had just become a graphic novel. I didn't know whether to be psyched as any fangirl would be, or to cry. *I really wished I had stayed at Grazi's for that extra cup of cocoa. Damn it!*

Clearly the stranger in black was there to help me, right? But I didn't know for sure. What if he was some kind of demon half-breed looking for a love slave! *Like, really Angela, get a grip!* And if he wanted a love slave, he could totally have me, I mean he was that hot. No, but seriously, I was freaking myself out for no reason.

The car made a wheezing sound and a second later the engine died, the headlights with it. At just about the same time clouds passed overhead and covered the moon almost completely. For a moment, we were in almost total darkness. If it wasn't for his eyes, which glowed a little bit, I swear he would've been invisible to me. *Witch.* My senses were tingling with the knowledge.

He was a Witch, that was for sure, but whether he was good, or evil wasn't so clear to me. I sat perfectly still. With any luck he'd forget I was there. Oh yeah, like I was easy to miss with my bright hair, and well, everything else.

"Step out of the car, Miss Tanner."

I sat dumbly and waited. Where the heck was my driver? I knew that he was supposed to protect me, but he wasn't doing such a bang-up job.

"I have no patience for this," he moved towards me and in a couple of quick efficient moves, he had me unbuckled and standing in front of him.

"Who—"

"My name is Jody Nieves. I'm a Guardian. You need to come with me."

2

CASTING MAGIC

He grabbed me by my arm and marched off into the darkness leaving me no room to refuse. What choice did I have anyway? Sure it was a ten-minute drive to the house, but it was freezing, pitch black, my car was totaled and my driver vanished.

I had no idea how long it would take me to get home if I walked by myself. Besides I'm a Witch and I know exactly what's out there in the darkness and, no thank you very much!

He was much taller than me, by at least ten inches. I had to take two steps for every one he took. I stumbled once, then twice. That was it!

"Hey! Do you mind? Some of us aren't ten feet tall!"

"What? Oh, sorry," he looked embarrassed and slowed his pace. I realized he was walking me straight into the woods and I had absolutely no control over the situation. My head swam with a million horrifying things that could happen to me, the least of which was being murdered. I was starting to hyperventilate, so instead of being scared I concentrated on being angry.

Where the heck was he taking me anyway? He could take that Man-of-Few-Words crap and just get lost. I mean, what was I supposed to do just follow him meekly and obey? No way!

"Okay look, Jody, right? You said you were a Guardian? That's like a protector for the white Covens, right? So why are dragging me into the woods in the middle of the night?"

"Miss Tanner, I was instructed by the Tribunal to get you and take you to the *meeting place*. Please wait until we arrive to ask your questions."

I grumbled at that, but he ignored me. In fact, I think he smirked. *The jerk!* I wished I remembered to grab my iPhone. It was unusual for me to go for more than ten minutes without being plugged in or logged on to something.

I spent a lot of time with *NewsFlash* and other online endeavors. That was the SHPS e-newsletter that I co-wrote and edited with a few other students. I also logged onto *WolfMoon* religiously and I was a member of several other online communities, social media, e-book clubs, developer chatrooms, etc.

Anyway, it was dark. I was cold and I was being dragged through the woods against my will by some huge Guardian who was as annoying as he was cute. I might not have mentioned this, but I was getting pretty boy crazy the past year. Unfortunately, chubby gingers were out of vogue at the moment. *C'est la vie.*

I made up for it with brains and personality, and my amazing ability to not give a crap. Take Mr. Tall, dark, and not so talkative here. He wouldn't give me the time of day if he wasn't ordered to take me to some meeting place.

Holy crap! Why the heck was I being summoned to a meeting place to begin with? It was almost the middle of the night, I was just attacked by some eyeless thing, I was in a car accident, and I was being kidnapped! Why me? I mean I didn't even know if I had powers yet. What was going on?

I had to bite my tongue to keep from lashing out. Prudent on my part, after all this guy had some serious skills as he just demonstrated by vanquishing that *thing*. After a few minutes of tromping through the cold forest my teeth started chattering. I was wearing a simple pair of brown leggings and a thin ivory sweater that came down to mid-thigh. My scarf and wool coat were back at the car. *Great.*

The self-proclaimed Guardian let go of my arm and I felt something warm surround me. He draped his jacket around my shoulders. It was larger than it looked and still warm from his body. Oh, and it smelled really, really good. Like woodsy aftershave, but I recognized it as his *anima magicae.*

"Thanks," I murmured.

"You're cold. I'm not. It's simple as that."

Well, there went all my warm and cozy feelings. *Jerk.* I rolled my eyes and almost missed a fallen branch, but he tugged me out of the way, and we walked around it. *Great, guess I'm the jerk.*

A few very long, very quiet minutes passed and still I kept my mouth shut. We walked by a couple of bare branched beech trees, the moon was shining again, and I wondered a bit at the pale bark. They looked like ghosts of trees. I guess they were sort of. No life in them as far as I could see, not a hint of it remained on the frozen surface.

I bumped into something solid and looked up; it was Jody's back. *Oops.* He was looking straight ahead at what appeared to be a wall of solid rock. Only it wasn't.

I could feel energy in the air. It was pulsating. Like

a slow and steady throb mimicking a human heartbeat, but much, much slower. There was no sound, no scent, nothing beyond the rock wall. It was as if that particular area of woods had been scrubbed clean by some super hazmat team or something.

I heard about places like this when I was very small. My father and the odd babysitter had told me of the "clean places" where magic was practiced in secret and Witches were governed by their own. This was the kind of thing that made scary bedtime stories for little Witches who didn't follow the rules. I dug my heels into the frozen ground.

Jody didn't seem to notice. He stood beside me and raised his left hand, revealing a scar that looked like it had been burned on the inside of his palm. It was in the shape of the pentacle, the five-pointed star inside of a circle that symbolized our Wiccan faith. It was a little tricky being both Wiccan and Christian, but I did okay.

He spoke in a clear strong voice and even though I knew I was being silly and romantic it made my heart thud a little louder in my chest.

·   ·   ·

"Air, Fire, Water, Earth,
      I call upon you elements here,
      Allow us passage thence,
Keep our hearts free from fear,
Hide our steps and scents,
In the name of the holy saints,
God and the Goddess,
Heaven and Earth,
As I will it so mote it be."

His spell was eloquent and simple. Not frightening like the cold light that had come from him before. He tugged on my arm and we walked through the invisible field of energy that had been designed to stop us, like a force field. I am not sure what would have happened had he not said his spell, but I can't imagine it would have been good.

We continued through the rock wall and despite the darkness we had no problem keeping to the path. I shivered. It was much too cold for Thanksgiving in New Jersey. His leather jacket was warm, but my face was frozen stiff. We rounded a bend and what I saw stopped me in my tracks. My eyes wide, I threw my head back and I screamed.

I moved to run forward, but something held me back. Big strong arms lifted me off of the ground and no matter how I struggled I couldn't break free. I even kicked my feet and I could swear I hit him, but he held me firmly in his grasp.

"Calm down. *Shhh*. It's okay, Angela, stop, stop, it's okay," the Guardian whispered in my ear.

"What? No! Dad!! Let me go, you—! Dad!?" Didn't he know that was my father in chains? They had him stripped down to his undershirt and pants with no socks or shoes on his feet in the freezing cold. He looked terrible.

"Just wait," Jody's cool breath tickled my neck, but I tried my best to ignore it.

"Angela Tanner?" A stern voice that I did not recognize called my name.

In fact, I hadn't even noticed the short, squat man who seemed to hover between standing and floating in a crimson robe behind my father. In his hands he held a long wooden staff. It was highly polished, and a dark stone sat on the top, it looked as if it was held there by nothing at all save the will of the Witch who held it.

"Your father, Francis Archibald Tanner, has agreed to confess to the crime of thievery. The stolen item is the Naga Amulet. It was unlawfully taken from fellow Witch, Sandor Blum. It once belonged to his mother and is the store for her powers, which her son was due to inherit during the next Solstice celebration thereby extending the crime to include magic stealing. These are grievous and heinous crimes for which your father will be executed according to our laws—"

"No!" the words escaped from my mouth before I could stop them. I knew what it meant to interrupt one of the Coven elders, but I couldn't help myself. Jody gave me a squeeze and I was oddly comforted.

"Silence, child, let me finish. He will be executed unless the amulet is returned to its rightful owner. You will have twenty-four hours."

"But, but why would he confess—"

"You have five minutes to speak with your father. Then he will be taken away."

Jody let me go and I ran toward my father. He was trembling and he looked worse than I had ever seen him. There were bags under his eyes and his hair looked like he had run his fingers through it a million times.

"Dad? What are they talking about?"

"Angela, there isn't any time. Look, I think maybe Kailey took the amulet."

"Mom? Why would she?" I stopped myself

before I finished. Mom was vain and selfish. It wasn't that farfetched to think she could do something like that. And my poor dad would willingly cover up for her. But execution? No way. This was way too serious.

"Angela, I'm sorry. I just didn't know what else to do. Just find her and tell her what's going on and make her bring it back, okay? I'm sorry, I'm so sorry."

I threw my arms around his neck, but I was flung backwards and landed with a hard thud on my butt in the frozen dirt. He was technically under arrest and there was no way I would be allowed to hug him. I wished I had my powers already so I could blast that stupid elder!

Okay, calm down, Angela. Think. I need Mom. I gotta get home.

I stood up as they dragged my father away and fought back tears. He nodded at me and mouthed *I love you.*

"I love you too, dad. I'll find Mom, don't worry!"

One second, he was in front of me, and the next he was gone. *Poof. Like magic.* And suddenly I was alone except for the Guardian skulking behind me. *Just great.* What were they gonna do? Strand me there?

I started walking as quickly as I could, and let's face it, I'm not so quick. Worse than that I had no sense of direction. As if he read my mind Jody tugged on my shoulder and pointed.

"It's that way."

I changed course and began stomping my way through the woods. *Stupid selfish cow!* She may be my mom, but we've never seen eye to eye. Truthfully, I didn't even think she liked me.

I used to feel bad about it, but oh well; I learned to accept looks had a lot more importance for her than they did me. Guess that's why I buried myself in my *NewsFlash* and gaming.

I couldn't hear the Guardian, but I knew he was keeping pace with me. Moving silently through the woods like some sort of ninja stalker. *Dude, come on?*

"Look, I don't know why you are following me. You arrested my dad and got him to confess to some crime he didn't commit. Even if I find the amulet, which I doubt, my mom should be the one you are looking for, not me!"

His dark eyebrows furrowed together, but he remained silent. After a few more minutes of walking we came to the street where we had crashed. My car and driver were nowhere in sight. I had a minor moment of panic when I noticed a sleek black motorcycle hidden behind a large walnut tree.

"Is that yours?" At his nod, I headed over to it.

"Wait a minute, I'm not giving you my bike—"

"Oh, really? You just stole my dad from me and set me off on this insane quest! I think the least you can do is drive me home!" I even stomped my foot. Temper tantrums were kind of a thing of mine back when I was a kid, of course I hadn't resorted to tactics like that since I was eight, but right then I was willing to do anything. *Silly, I know, but hey, a girl's gotta do...*

He looked confused for a moment. I have to admit he was pretty hot standing there under the dull streetlight. It gave him a sort of otherworldly glow. He looked up and down the street making sure no one was in the area. Then he lifted his hand, the one with the scar, and the motorcycle, a Ducati Streetfighter custom painted a matte black, stood up on its own then drove itself over to us.

It was glowing a little with the magic he used to manipulate the truly awesome piece of machinery. No doubt, I would have appreciated it more had I not been worrying about my father's fate at that moment. *What the hell did my mom do?*

"Okay, here, strap this to your head and hold onto my waist," he sat down on the bike, his helmet already in place. He looked me over then handed me a helmet, which he seemed to pull out of thin air. *Nice trick.*

"Zip up the jacket."

I grabbed the helmet, slapped it over my curls, zipped up my borrowed leather jacket and got on behind him with a heck of a lot more confidence than I felt.

We made it to my house in under two minutes. My face was frozen, but what a ride! I jumped off the bike and thrust the helmet at him. I walked up the long driveway to the double front doors of my house. Montville was full of large homes just like mine, but not all of them had an entire orchard growing behind them.

I heard Jody's low whistle and I cringed on the inside. Daddy made money. Lots of it. And Mom, well, she liked to show it off. Our home was maybe just a little bit ostentatious. Okay, it was a lot ostentatious. What with our custom stucco siding, gilded fixtures, and the exquisite hand carved masonry depicting nature scenes with the sun, falling stars, rolling valleys of flowers and trees, ocean waves, clouds, and flames forever frozen in stone in each of the four enormous columns that stood guard in front of our house. One for earth, one for air, one for water, and one for fire.

We also had ornamental Japanese cherry trees and maples, slate stone walkways, three water fountains, a koi pond, a gazebo and numerous outdoor amenities that weren't visible in the winter. Jody kept pace just behind me and I tried not to care about his reactions to the outside of my home. After all, it only got worse inside.

We had seven bedrooms, eight bathrooms, an indoor swimming pool, a private screening room, a game room with a custom pool and billiards table, a marble chess table with hand carved pieces in the shapes of supernatural creatures, an enormous crystal chandelier, polished hardwood floors, hand carved Mahogany doors, a dining room that seated twenty-five comfortably, a state of the art kitchen, and an elevator that went straight to the master bedroom.

I rarely came into the main house anymore unless Dad was home. I had my own private entrance around the side. There was a private stairway that went to my suite of rooms, which included a bedroom, master bathroom, guest room, guest bathroom, a mini kitchen, a living room with a sweet plush couch in green velvet, which I actually designed, and my pride and joy, my workstation.

I am a gamer so naturally I have just about every new techie toy there is from a seventy-inch ultra HD LED Smart TV, to my Wii, Xbox One, PlayStation, the latest MacBook, a custom PC, a few tablets, both

Android and Mac, and an entire wall of flat screen monitors. I spent *a lot* of time online.

It was embarrassing. The money that is. You see, most Witches practiced Wicca and were more in tune with nature and going green than they were with all this monetary gain. I mean sure, Witches made money, some were good at it. Dad certainly was. He had a knack for it, but he tried to balance his success at work with his beliefs by keeping his orchard and donating funds to charity. Mom had no real skills. I mean, she was good at looking good and spending Dad's money. Then there was me. I grew up with a lot of money, so it wasn't a big deal for me. I suppose I was spoiled, but I never really looked at it like that.

When I was little my mom would hire nannies to take me shopping and get my hair done, but I never really cooperated with what they thought was in style. So, I gave up on being her idea of beautiful a long time ago. I mostly used my allowance to splurge on all my tech toys and I admit I do have a thing for clothes and shoes. Hey, I like to shop; I'm a teenager. It's in my DNA. I mean, I'm not exactly goth, rockabilly, steampunk, pin-up or preppy. I'm more like a healthy mix of all the above. Like Jaden Smith, I wore what was comfortable, what spoke to me, what I liked. The hell with the rest of them.

I ignored Jody's second whistle as he looked over the outside of my house and went for the security keypad near the front door. Any normal or Witch wanting entry would have to know the secret pass code, as well as the correct incantation for the spell I had rigged into the wiring. It took me a few tries, but I had managed to incorporate a protection spell into the lock mechanism itself. Genius, right? Anyway, I looked at Jody and shrugged. I could change it later.

The pass code was 13,15,18,14, and 26. My dad told me once they were all important dates, the 14th was my birthday, the 18th was his, but Mom's was the 23rd and it wasn't there. He never told me what the rest stood for. I focused on the lock itself and murmured the words I had chosen to unlock the spell.

"East, West, North and South,
    The coast is clear, friend, no fear,
    I bid you open with my mouth,
I come with good intentions here,
All is well, truthfully,
As I will so mote it be."

. . .

"Impressive spell casting for someone who hasn't come into her powers yet," Jody spoke from behind me. I had to concentrate not to react to his deep voice. It sort of tickled my ear.

"Yeah, well, any fool can write a rhyme."

I shrugged my shoulder and opened the door. I wasn't expecting the compliment, but I couldn't focus on that. I needed to find my mom and ask her about the amulet. I pushed open the door wide and motioned for Jody to enter. His dark eyes went wide as I knew they would. The entryway made an impression as it was designed to.

The floors were polished, and the marble fireplace glowed with the soft light of a dying fire. I wondered why dad left it on. The turned over chair in front of his desk in the large office to our right reminded me that he hadn't exactly planned on leaving tonight. He was taken. And he had confessed! I straightened my shoulders and began calling for my mom. She needed to fix this!

"Mom! Mom! Where are you?"

The house was empty. I knew it even as I ran from room to room. I jumped on the personal elevator, Jody hot on my heels and pushed the 'up' button. I normally never went into my mom's and dad's bedroom. I mean, *yuck*, why would I? Besides my mother never wanted me around much.

"Mom!"

When the elevator doors opened, I immediately noticed that something was wrong. The bed was unmade, drawers were open and emptied onto the hand woven Persian area rug. Papers were scattered from my father's nightstand, shoes strewn about. And the walk-in closet looked like a tornado hit it.

"Whoa."

"Mom?" I hated the tears I heard in my voice.

I walked to the dresser and found her jewelry box opened and dumped out. Nothing appeared to be missing, but I couldn't be sure. The wall safe was open and stacks of money were falling out of it, some jewelry and paperwork too, but I couldn't tell if anything was missing.

"Blum's men have already searched here."

"Yeah, but if they found something the Tribunal wouldn't still have my dad."

"Exactly what I was thinking," Jody walked over to a section of the bedroom that had been thoroughly explored. He placed his head on the wall and closed his eyes.

"There is something here. Behind this panel."

I knew what it was, but I wasn't sure I could trust

him. I thought of my dad cold and alone with that horrible Witch about to pay for a crime he didn't commit and shook off whatever trepidation I had. I walked over to the wall and touched the left corner of the bookcase that sat in front of the panel. A keypad opened up and I began typing the pass code that would grant me access to the panic room my dad had installed in case of an emergency.

The wall slid open and we were met by a steel door. Magic barred entrance to the room once it had been activated and clearly someone had activated it. The door glowed an unearthly blue and the hum of power was loud in the confined space. I didn't dare touch the door.

"Mom! Mom!" I screamed until I was almost hoarse. The small video monitor lit up and I saw my mom in all her blonde glory with mascara stains down her face and handfuls of jewels and clothing in her arms. Like she had grabbed whatever she could and ran for the panic room.

"Angela? Is that you?"

"Yeah. Mom, it's me! Look they've got dad!"

"Oh my Goddess! Angela they, they ruined everything! Look at my house! Look at my things! What's going to happen?"

"Mom! For real?! Shut up and listen to me, open the door!"

"Who is that with you? Oh no, my face! Is my hair okay? Turn around young man, please, I—I'm not at my best right now—"

"Mom!! They have dad! Do you know where the amulet is?"

"Wh—What amulet? How could they do this? My things!" I could tell by her pout and the way she was frantically wiping at her face and hair that she was more concerned with her appearance in front of the Guardian than she was with the imprisonment of her husband. *Oh boy, the Goddess save me from silly vain women.*

"Mom! Focus! They took dad because of some amulet, the Naga Amulet from the family Blum. They say you stole it, Mom!"

"What? Me? Steal it? No, no, no! Sandor gave me that amulet as a gift for, well, um, for, anyway it's not important why, he just did! I didn't steal anything!"

"Well, whatever Mom, I don't care why, but he wants it back and the Tribunal is charging dad with theft! It's punishable by death! Give it to me and I will bring it to them. Now open the door."

"Um, the thing is, Angela, I don't exactly have it anymore. I, um, well, I traded it."

"You traded it? For what?"

"Look, there are things I needed to stay who I am. Archie knew that when we got married," I watched her speak as if she were a total stranger.

Her tears dried up pretty quickly when I said dad was the one in trouble. I wished for a moment it was her instead. Guilt made my stomach turn.

"Mom, come with me, let's talk to them and tell them it was a gift—"

"Oh, uh, I don't think I should do that. Your father wouldn't want to see me in jail."

"How am I even related to you?" I couldn't believe she was this unfeeling for my father, *her husband*.

"Funny you should mention that." She brushed back her blonde hair and looked directly into the camera, her expression was cold.

"Look, Angela, I've tried to be a good parent to you, but motherhood isn't exactly for me. It never was. Archie and I tried, but he knew I was going to leave someday. He wants to grow old and be grandparents to your kids. I mean, really? Let me tell you, at first, I laughed it off. I mean what are the chances of *you* getting married? I mean realistically. You were a chubby little carrot top, Angela, it was nothing personal. I just figured I didn't have to worry about all that, but as you've grown older, I tell you, it's been a worry," She paced a little and re-adjusted her bra, smoothing down the lines of her disheveled shirt. I could only watch as the woman I called mom unraveled before my eyes.

"It's simple really, I was not made for parenthood! I am certainly not grandma material! I told him. I told Archie. He knows this! I want excitement! Money, jewelry, champagne, traveling, not PTA meetings and, and cookie sales! Still I stayed! I put in my twelve years and damn it, *I* want something out of this marriage! Archie just couldn't understand, could he? He thought I'd change. Doesn't he know that people never really change? Not *really* inside where it counts," she looked at the camera with big blue eyes and a face that said how could anyone not agree with her?

"Anyway, I am what I am. Promises of eternal youth and beauty, excitement and adventure, and riches beyond imagination were enough to get me on board! What woman wouldn't want those things? So, yeah, I did it. I seduced Sandor Blum and he gave me the Naga Amulet. The fool. He thought I really cared for him. Men are so simple, so very simple. I didn't even have to work that hard. Hmm. Anyway, I couldn't get it back now if I tried. It's too late, I—I gave the amulet to Hector Desearo and he gave me this," she held up a glass potion bottle containing a sluggish green liquid.

"It's mine and I won't give it back. One more week for potency and I'll have everything I have ever wanted."

My mouth hung open as I listened to her go on and on. *Stop.* I wanted to scream it from the top of my lungs. *How could she?* The way she stared at the potion bottle as if it were precious to her was sickening. *Why didn't I tell her to shut up?* I guess I needed to hear it. All of it. *Twelve years? But I'll be seventeen in a few months. She seduced Mr. Blum? She cheated on Dad! Hector Desearo, I knew that name, but from where?*

It registered then that the door to the panic room remained locked. She made no move to open it. Funny how that was what brought me out of my trance.

"You're not my mother." It was a fact. I knew I should be sad or hurt, but mostly, I felt relieved. At least I could understand why she had treated me the way she did all those years. *Not my mother.*

My guilt at never measuring up to her expectations, the years of pain and loneliness, all of them were for nothing. I always thought she was perfect, beautiful, but I suddenly realized her beauty was an illusion. I turned around and walked away from the woman who was not my mother.

I couldn't look at Jody. His face was somber and full of pity. I didn't want that. Not from him. In fact, I couldn't stand the idea of it. I left the shambles of my parents', *no*, my *dad's* room behind me and took the elevator downstairs. I entered my private apartments and headed for my laptop.

I pretended not to notice Jody standing behind me, but of course I knew he was there. His magic was cold and bright, not exactly welcoming or friendly, but still I trusted him not to harm me. I began searching through my father's email. It took seconds for me to hack my way into his personal files.

He really had no idea how good I was on a computer and he thought he had the best in the business working for him. It didn't matter though. I could break through any screen protectors, firewalls, or anti-hacking tools that I had come across. It seemed to help when I hummed to myself when I was typing.

I searched and searched and finally, after hacking into his public relations files, I came across a picture from a local e-magazine of my dad, the woman I thought was my mom, and Hector Desearo. My father was smiling in that charming way he had, his dark hair and square chin made him look something like George Clooney, definitely dreamboat material, and Kailey, well she was stunning in a skintight red dress, her golden hair flowed over one perfectly tanned bare shoulder, and then there was Mr. Desearo.

He had a certain elegance in the way he carried himself. He was shorter than my dad, stouter too, but still he was handsome, with his thick brown hair, tanned skin and black eyes. His aura was different though. I could sense it even through the image. My dad was affable, kind, sincere. Mr. Desearo looked hard, ruthless even. What was my dad doing with him?

The caption under the image explained it all. They were at a charity event that took place just last month at the Desearo Spanish Heritage Museum of Northern New Jersey. That made sense. My dad supported many local museums and art galleries. So, nope, not unusual for him to be acquaintances with a man like that. No, what caught my eye was the showcase behind the trio that sported a glass covered display of necklaces of various materials and lengths, each sporting a large pendant or amulet.

"Jody! Look!"

3

I pointed at the screen and Jody leaned down over me. He smelled like good. Clean and light like snow. I rubbed my nose and ignored the way my heart quickened in my chest.

"What are you thinking?"

"I'm thinking this Desearo has the amulet, and he has it here," I tapped on the screen where the address of the museum was located.

"We can check it out in the morning, I guess. Don't look at me like that. You know we can't go now, it's too late. And we can't just break into a museum, Angela."

"Okay. I know. Um, just swing by in the morning or I can call you when I'm done."

"Um, no can do. I am to stay with you until this is done. Essentially, I am *your* Guardian for the time being."

"What?"

"Hey, I won't try anything, I'm duty sworn to protect you."

"Please, you don't have to say things like that. I'm aware you won't exactly have to restrain yourself around me," I got up from the computer and stalked across the room, taking off my sweater and my boots and throwing them into my closet. My t-shirt rode up my stomach a bit and I pulled it back down quick as I could. I was in no mood to have this guy pandering to my ego. After all it didn't take a rocket scientist to know a guy like that didn't go for girls like me.

I went to turn around and thudded into a hard chest. My eyes went wide as I saw the look on Jody's face. First off, he was not looking at my face, he was looking at my body, like totally, *looking* looking.

"Uh—"

"I'm not sure what kind of idiots have made you believe things like that about yourself. Maybe that bottle blonde stepmother of yours or some idiot teenage bullies at that school you go to, but Angela, there is something you need to know."

"What's that?"

"You are absolutely gorgeous."

"What did you say?" My words came out as a whisper. I was so close to him I could almost feel his power, only what felt cold to me before was warm and comforting and alive.

"I'm sorry, I shouldn't have called her your stepmom, I was only guessing from what she said—"

"Not about that. I'll deal with that later. What did you say, about me, being um, gorgeous?" I bit my bottom lip. It was bigger than my top lip and mom, I mean Kailey, always yelled at me when I bit it, but I couldn't help it. Nervous habit.

"*Oh, damn.* I'm sorry, but I just have to—" He moved in closer to me than I thought was possible.

His body was a breath away from mine. Not touching, but oh-so-close. My chest tightened and I held my breath as he reached out with his hands and took me by the neck and face. He brought his cool, soft lips down to mine in a kiss that I was so not expecting.

He tasted like Altoids, you know, the really strong peppermints that exploded in your mouth with such intense minty flavor that burned so good. *Mmm.* I took the step that brought my body right up against his and when I did, I swear I felt *him*. His *anima magicae*, that is, his power and energy hummed in the air all around us. Our lips remained locked and my red curls swirled around in a cool breeze that came from him. I felt tingles all along my skin.

"I shouldn't have done that," he pressed his forehead to mine as we both tried to catch our breaths. *Whoa.*

"That was, I mean, um, wow. By the Goddess, Angela, you taste like heaven and I would love nothing more than to keep kissing you, but I am here to protect you during your father's trials."

"No, I get it, um, let's just forget that happened," I couldn't quite meet his eyes. It wasn't my first kiss, but it was the first time anyone had ever made me feel like that. I needed time to process what was going on.

"No, I don't think I want to forget it even if I could. How about we re-visit it, after all this, deal? Good. Okay, I'm going to go to the guest room and keep watch from there. I've placed protection spells on all entrances and exits,"

"When did you do that?"

"While you were busy typing away over there on your computer. I never could work one of those things. Anyway, it's alright, we will be safe here tonight. If anything tries to get in here, I'll know it, okay? Now, get some sleep."

I stood in the doorway to my closet for a few

minutes after he left. *Holy crap. What the heck just happened?* I shook my head and reached for the dresser. I pulled on a pair of cozy flannel pajamas in hot pink with little black skulls with red bows all over them. Normally I wore the bottoms with a tank top, but I figured I better wear the actual pajama top with Jody walking around next door. *Jody, mmm.*

He kissed me! Really kissed me.

I could not get the feel of his kiss out of my head. The last time a boy had kissed me was at my school's Harvest Dance. My date was some prat wanting to intern at Daddy's offices. *He* kissed me, but it was kind of gross. He just shoved his tongue down my throat, and I wound up smacking him upside his head.

Jody kissed like I always imagined it could be. You know that sort of daydream kiss kids have when reading a book or watching a favorite movie. Like when Belle finally kisses Beast, or when Arwen and Aragorn embrace, or even when Bella and Edward kiss for the first time. Alright, yes, you got me, I am a *Twilight* fangirl and I am proud to be one!

Anyway, I couldn't believe everything that had just happened. I mean, I went from Thanksgiving dinner at my best friend's house to the freaking twilight zone! First things first, I pulled my back up iPhone out of my desk drawer and checked to make sure it was charged and hooked it up to my Verizon Wireless account. Then I sat back down at my computer and started gathering all the information I could on the museum and Desearo. I just hoped it would be enough.

I must have dozed off at some point because I woke up to someone shaking my arm and yelling my name. *Crap, I don't wanna wake up.* I was having the most delicious dream.

I was dancing under the moonlight and there was fire all around me, but I was safe and laughing and happy in Jody's arms. His dark eyes gazed into mine and we kissed, his icy mint breath met mine and it felt so cool, so good, then he lifted me up and he felt so strong and tall, and then— *splash*!

"What the heck!! Ahh!" I was in the shower. Icy cold water pelted down on me and I starred daggers at Jody who looked as if he had just seen a ghost!

"What the heck did you do that for?!"

"Angela! Are you okay?" He ran his hands over my body and turned me around looking at me from head to toe. It took me a minute to function but when I did, I pushed at him and yelled back. *What the heck?*

"What do you mean am *I* okay? You tried to drown me!"

"What? No! You were on fire!"

"What are you talking about I was dreaming!"

"Look! Just look!" he pointed to my body and I looked down. All I saw was soaking wet remnants of my flannel pajamas as they hung off my unharmed body in charred scraps of cloth.

"Ahh! What the—?! Well, get out, get out!" I screamed at him as I realized there was barely anything left to my pajamas and I was practically standing there naked!

"Look, I'll turn around, but only after I see you aren't hurt."

"I'm not! I swear, just wait outside, please."

"Fine," he ground out the answer between clenched teeth. He wasn't happy, but *hello*, I was soaking wet and covered in practically nothing but ash and pieces of burnt fabric.

"Didn't you hear me pounding on the door?" I heard Jody's question in spite of the running water and the closed bathroom door.

I used my special shampoo and conditioner made especially for me by Sherry. It was the best thing for my ultra-curly hair, and it smelled like lavender, rosemary and mint. It soothed me as I tried to figure out what had just happened.

"No. I really didn't hear anything. I was sleeping,"

I felt rather than heard him walk across the room. His footfalls were heavy and punctuated by the steel toed boots he wore. I finished getting washed and stuffed the remnants of my pajamas into the trashcan after ringing them out in the tub. I put on a thick terry cloth bathrobe and wrapped my hair up in a towel.

"Jody? Can you just give me a minute to get dressed please?"

"Huh? Yeah, sure. I'll stand outside the door."

I hurried into a pair of thick black leggings, warm knee high purple Uggs, and a huge matching purple sweater with an oversized cowl neck that sat snug over one shoulder. My hair was drying in its usual chaotic manner all over my head and shoulders. I applied some light lip gloss and mascara and opened the door to find Jody staring at it.

"Um, hi?"

"That was pretty fast."

"Yeah. I don't need hours for this look."

"However long it takes, it's worth it," he said looking at me with his smiling dark eyes. They turned serious when he looked at the chair I had fallen asleep on. It was slightly scorched. *Yikes.*

"Um, look I fell asleep in my chair while I was on my computer. I don't know what happened. I'm not hurt though, you know. Nothing is, um, burnt. Well, except my pajamas," I could feel my cheeks burning with embarrassment, and believe me blushing did not look good on a redhead. The more I wanted to stop, the worse it got. *Okay, deep breaths.*

Jody walked around the chair holding his hand out as he did so. His eyes were closed as he was focused on whatever he was doing. When he opened them, they glowed a light teal color as opposed to their natural dark tone. *Whoa.*

"Angela, I—I think you're a Fire Witch."

I had no response to his statement. I needed to think, but first I needed to figure out a way to save Dad. Jody and I walked back to the main part of the house. I went straight to my mom's, no, I mean my *step mom's* room with the intention of talking her out of the panic room. The problem was she was already gone.

"There's a note," Jody's voice was somber as he held the envelope out to me.

"No, you read it, please," I sat down on the edge of the unmade bed and waited as he cleared his throat. This was so awkward.

"'*Angela, Tell your father I tried, I really did. I signed the divorce papers that he gave to me the day we married, just in case I ever wanted out. Well, I want out and they are on his desk downstairs. I tried to be a mother to you, but I am just not cut out for it. We never did see eye to eye about you, his little angel. Ask him about your real mom. He never told me much about her. He just tried to do what he thought was best for you.*

I know I was not the faithful, devoted wife he wanted, but he knew what he was getting into the day he met me. Tell him I'm going to empty the cash from the safety deposit box. I will send an address where I want all my things shipped sometime in the future.

Desearo promised me eternal youth and adventure for the amulet, but I never collected the final ingredient for the potion he gave to me. He was supposed to hand it over when he drained the amulet; I guess he hasn't done that yet. That should make ownership of the amulet easier to establish since it was payment for services not rendered. Ask your Guardian, he will know what I mean.' It's signed Kailey."

I sat quietly for a moment. I only had a day left to clear my dad. I needed to go.

"Angela, are you okay?"

"Am I okay? Um, how about no! No, I'm not okay, my dad's been arrested for something that nitwit did and I have no idea if I can pull off saving him. Not to mention you think I may be a Fire Witch. A *Fire Witch*? Really! There hasn't been A Fire Witch in our Coven for hundreds of years. I used to hear stories about them when I was a kid! What the heck does it mean anyway?" I ran my hair through my red curls and stomped towards the elevator. Jody remained silent beside me as we headed downstairs. I could feel his thoughtful concern, but I was feeling too raw to acknowledge it.

"Look, it's not that bad, right? I mean, I thought she was *my mother*. And I always thought there was something really wrong with me. I mean, I don't look like her, I never cared about following the latest fashion trends or Hollywood diets or the stupid Kardashians. I mean, for years I blamed myself for why we never seemed to have any relationship, but at least now I know it's not my fault, you know. It's actually a relief."

"That's wise, truly. You're smarter and braver than I thought and that's saying something. But Angela, even if she was your biological mother, there is not and there never was anything wrong with you. You got that?" His dark eyes glowed an icy teal for a moment and he looked at me with an intensity I had never experienced.

I mean all the boys I knew were just that, *boys*. Even Derek, my most recent crush. And he was just beautiful! He worked as a soda jerk at my favorite hangout, Cybersodas. It was an Internet café/old-timey malt shoppe. He was super cute too, with his tanned skin, hazel green eyes, and outrageously curly hair. I thought he was perfect then and that was before I knew that he played *WolfMoon*. Seriously, perfect guy for me, right? Well, even *he* seemed juvenile and silly next to the powerful Witch standing in front of me.

I looked down at our feet to stop myself from staring at his face. His skin was smooth and darker than mine, olive toned as opposed to my stark ivory, and his hair was dark and wavy and fell to his chin. He had full lips and intense brown eyes. *Talk about beautiful.* It took some effort, but I managed not to reach out and brush his hair back with my hands.

Looking down I continued my comparison. He wore steel-toed leather biker boots and I had on my purple sweater Uggs. They couldn't be more different, and yet they seemed to complement each other. I wondered if we would too. He seemed to smile at me, and I laughed a little too. *Way to break the ice.*

"So, why do you think I'm a Fire Witch? You know, besides the obvious."

"Well, just look at *you*."

"What do you mean?"

"First off, Fire Witches were renowned for their beauty and for their trademark red hair and ivory skin. Their power was unmatched."

"But I don't even have a talent yet!"

"Angela, your eyes have changed shade every few minutes since you woke up this morning. That's a mark of power. I think you have more talent than you know. When I found you this morning you were *on fire* and completely unharmed. I have never been so terrified and amazed in my entire life and I've been a Guardian for over five years now."

"But I didn't do anything. I was just dreaming."

"That reminds me, what were you dreaming about?"

"Oh, um, nothing, I mean, I don't remember really," I was so not telling him that I dreamt of being in his arms after he had kissed me last night. Or that in my dream we were dancing and laughing surrounded by flames. He'd think I was nuts and I needed to be mature about this. *But a Fire Witch, hmm.* I'd have to talk to Sherry, my mentor, about it after all this was over. I needed to get my father back.

I grabbed a North Face jacket from the hall closet and a pair of thick gloves with a matching neck warmer. I offered Jody his pick of my dad's gloves, but he smiled and said he was fine in the cold. Considering his magic I could understand that.

Without reservation I jumped on the back of his Ducati and held on as we headed for Desearo's museum. It was just after eight o'clock in the morning, the website said they would open at nine. I knew we would be there when it did.

4

The Desearo Spanish Heritage Museum of Northern New Jersey was located in Morristown. It was a twenty-minute ride down Route 287 from my home in Montville, but then again everything seemed to be about twenty minutes away, give or take.

I liked going to Morristown. It was large and diverse, full of great restaurants and shops, and it had significant historical value. The town played a pretty important role in the American Revolution according to my history teachers. Over the years I had been on plenty of trips to places like Jockey Hollow, Fosterfields Living Historical Farm, Acorn Hall, the Arboretum, and the Morris Museum. The Morristown St.

Patrick's Day parade was one of my all-time favorite events of the year.

Most of those trips were organized by my school, but a few had been with Sherry or my dad. A lot of the older farms and gardens still grew plants that were vital to many of our Coven's ceremonies and practices. Most modern Covens have deals with farms like these. They let us pick what we need, and we include their continued growth and health in our services. It's symbiotic.

Jody drove his motorcycle like a bat out of hell. The biting winter wind whipped around us, but I was neither cold nor scared. In fact, I loved it! The speed and the feel of the motorcycle beneath me gave me a rush. I can't lie, I also loved the feel of my body pressed up as close as I could get against his.

My arms wrapped tightly around his waist. I don't know whether it was exhilaration or adrenaline, all I know was I could feel his abs, rock hard, underneath my gloved hands. He was big. Not fat at all, though not what I would call skinny. He was taller and more muscular than most male Witches I had met. I almost felt petite sitting behind him that way and that was saying something. I guess being a Guardian was physically demanding, like being a firefighter or something. Only he put out magical fires so to speak.

I get that I'm bigger than most girls my age. I can't shop in half the teen stores at the local mall. They just don't have clothes for girls built like me, but I manage just fine with Etsy and Wanelo. It has been a long road for me to learn to love my body. I still have my moments when doubt and insecurity sink in. I mean really, who doesn't?

Grazi once told me I looked like I belonged in the 1950s. At first, I admit I was a little upset by the remark. She explained herself by saying she had always been tall and skinny her entire life. She grew up being teased by her cousins and ignored by boys. I was totally floored when she said she always wanted to be a bit more curvy, like me. I guess part of that came from growing up with her grandmother and watching lots of old movies too. The women in those films looked a lot different than today's Hollywood ideal.

I wasn't jealous or bitter about my weight and that's pretty much the entire battle, right? I mean, look, I have oodles of curves. No matter what I do, I never seem to get any thinner than a size nine, though an eleven seems to be my typical size. To a lot of girls in my school that means I am obese. Sure it hurts my feelings, but hey, I have learned to love myself. All of me. And I don't care what everyone else thinks.

I was never so comfortable in my skin as I was at that very moment with the world passing me by at incredible speeds on the back of Jody's bike. He actually made me feel small-ish. That didn't happen all that often. I'd have loved to think about him and me and where we were going to go with this *thing* that I felt between us, but I had other things on my mind. Still, I was picking up on some seriously good vibes from him. Whether that was because I am a Witch or not, I'm not sure. I didn't know much about him, but he was helping me and that counted for something.

We had just passed the famous Morristown Green when I saw the museum. The Green is the heart of Morristown. It is the site where the courthouse and jail stood during the Revolutionary War, and it was the burial site for soldiers during the winter of 1777 when Washington and his troops camped there.

I was always sensitive to places with a past, you know, historical hot spots that had seen a lot of action or drama. This place made my skin buzz with leftover energy. Only certain Witches saw ghosts and so far, I was not one of them, but if I could, I bet I'd see a whole lot of them in the Morristown Green.

The museum looked small on the outside. The old

brick building was on the corner of North Park Place. I think it used to be an old department store. There was not much that a person, even a Witch, could do about the outside façade of buildings in Morristown. They had to follow certain rules and criteria to keep up the historical appearance.

I heard Jody speak softly under her breath and I realized he had created a small parking space for his motorcycle right in front of the building. *Cool*. I got off first and handed him my helmet. He took his off and in the blink of an eye both helmets were gone. Placed in some sort of magical invisible storage hold.

I was raised knowing full well what I am, but each Witch had different gifts of varying strengths. Sure charms and such were kept in *spell books* and passed down and shared, but some magic was purely derived from the individual Witch. The strongest White Witches usually held spots of authority in a Coven or were employed as Guardians, Keepers of Law, Spells, or Magic Stores, and Trainers.

Jody was a Guardian. Sherry was a Trainer. The elder I had met, who was part of the Tribunal against my dad, was a Keeper of the Law. Most Witches went through life without being noticed, even by their Covens, but some, some were special.

Dark Witches were usually more powerful because

of the blood sacrifices they practiced. They were odious crimes for which they would be punished either by the demons they sought to control or the power they tried to harness. We had little to do with Dark Covens.

Guardians were secretive about their talents. Jody was showing me an immeasurable amount of trust when he used magic in front of me. Spell casting, or just Casting, as Witches tended to call it, was a very personal thing. In the old days it was also cause for jealousy and treachery. Dark Witches would follow particularly talented White Witches and kill them for their magic. I don't know how this was done, I just know that as a result Guardians were appointed to protect and sort out magical disputes.

I nodded at Jody in appreciation of his trust. He tipped his leonine head slightly in my direction. His dark hair blew around his face, the cold wind felt worse here than it had when we were on his Ducati. That was strange, but I was too focused on the intensity of his dark eyes to pay it any more attention than that.

He made me feel warm inside. Like, *really warm.* It was a strange and new feeling. I didn't quite know how to react, so I took my iPhone out of my pocket and went through the motions of shutting off the ringer and quickly checking my texts. This wasn't the time or place to get butterflies over a boy.

Desearo was a strong Witch from the info I gathered from my dad's files. He wouldn't take this little intrusion into his museum lightly. I needed to be smart and alert. For the first time since seeing my dad carted off in chains I was frightened. Really frightened. I guess I'd be a fool not to be.

The thing about accusing a Witch of wrongdoing was there could be serious repercussions. You see, without proof, said Witch could kill you on the spot and it would be deemed justifiable. Witches had certain rules and laws, most of which were based in the old 'do no harm' adage, however according to our laws insults were still considered offences punishable by death. Witches used to duel all the time over what was really nothing more than name-calling. Silly? Maybe. Petty? Possibly. But I wasn't one to judge.

Besides like my dad was always telling me, there was a lot of good to be said for our ways too. After all we were caretakers, nurturers, growers, healers. The world benefited from us and we from it. A *partnership* that began eons ago.

The brick building looked cold. Empty. I wondered at just what we would find inside. Witches did have day jobs, but a museum curator? How dangerous could he be? I tried to fit the picture I had of Desearo from that article with his title, but I came up short. He didn't look like a museum curator or owner, or even anyone who liked museums. What was he really doing inside there?

I felt better with Jody by my side, but still I wasn't ready to be responsible for his death either. With that in mind we entered the museum and were greeted by the smell of floor cleaner and gas heat.

It felt good to get out of the cold, but that kind of dry air was liable to make my hair frizz. *Ugh.* I smiled at the middle-aged guard and walked over to the counter where a young woman was waiting with a bright smile on her face. Her name tag said Yolanda.

"Hola Yolanda, dos entradas por favor," Jody eased in front of me and held out a slightly crumbled twenty-dollar bill. His Spanish was said with the ease of a native speaker.

He handed the giggling Yolanda a twenty-dollar bill and I watched as they continued back in forth in rapid Spanish that was much too fast for me to even try to understand. Okay, I'll admit it, I was jealous. Even more so when she dismissed me with half a glance. Clearly, she didn't see me as competition.

After all, she was petite and thin with her long brown hair pulled back into some fancy up-do that my hair would never, ever stay in. She had liquid black eyes and plump red lips and a smile that said she liked what she saw. So basically, she was my polar opposite.

I looked like a chubby Q-tip that someone set on fire with my pale skin and bright hair by comparison. Her tan skin blushed prettily as she bit her lip and looked Jody up and down. She clearly welcomed more attention from him.

"Okay, thank you very much, *Yolanda*," I grabbed the tickets and the change from her and hurried inside pulling Jody along with me. He smiled and linked our hands and I felt a jolt all the way to my stomach. *Not now, Angela.* But still I grinned and squeezed his hand in mine.

Inside, the museum was dark. There were soft lights in the display cases, but the rest of the room was not very well lit. It made it pretty difficult to see where we were going. I tried to recall the photo I had seen of my father and Desearo.

I had a pretty good memory. In seconds I had the image clear in my mind. They were standing in front of a large glass case that was backlit against a marble column with glittering gold veins. That was the case we needed to find. It had been full of necklaces with unique pendants.

"Angela, look here," Jody pointed to the brochure

in his hand, "It says there are over 300 paintings from South America and Mexico on display here, as well as a significant amount of jewelry dating as far back to the 13th century."

"Does it say where the jewelry is?"

"Second floor."

We looked at each other and I shrugged. A snatch and grab would have been easier on the first floor, but something told me this was not going to be easy. There was an elevator, but Jody looked uncomfortable with the tiny metal box, so we opted for the stairs.

We seemed to be the only two people on the first floor who didn't work there. I imagined the upstairs would be just as deserted at this time of day.

It was. We exited the tiny stairwell to find a similarly decorated second floor. Gold letters decorate an exposed brick wall when we entered. It read *"Joyas de Espana, America del Sur, y Mexico"*

"Joyas means jewelry," Jody spoke softly, but still I jumped. My senses were in overdrive.

"Thanks," I answered as I looked around the front of the room only to find we were alone.

"Let's start here," Jody tugged on our still linked hands and we began walking up and down, aisle after aisle. We saw broaches, hair combs, cufflinks, watches, rings, tiaras, earrings, elaborate *collardas* which were large necklaces of intricate design made out of pure silver, and tiny bejeweled dolls which kind of gave me the creeps.

Everything we saw was made of the purest gold and silver. The European influences were in the precious gemstones. I had never seen such large emeralds, sapphires, rubies, pearls, and diamonds. The Native jewelry favored turquoise, coral, and amber. Both styles were beautiful, but the closer we got to the end of the room the dizzier I began to feel.

It was like the walls were closing in on me. My heartbeat was loud in my ears and I could hear each breath go in and out of my nose and then my mouth. I didn't normally get sick, but I felt like I was suddenly coming down with the flu. I felt woozy, uncomfortable. I was trembling and a little bit nauseous.

"Stop, I—I need a minute," I lifted a hand to my head and realized I had broken out in a sweat. Jody let go of my hand and placed his on my temple.

"You feel okay, no fever, but your eyes are a bit glassy."

"No, I know. I mean, I feel, like, a little dizzy, like this part of the room is making me sick."

"Hmm, I think you're right. I didn't notice it. I mean, it's really subtle, but there is an unusual amount of energy flowing through this space," he followed me with his dark eyes as if he was searching for something.

"You said before that you didn't know you were on fire, and you haven't developed your talents yet, but you just picked up a vein of magic that I had missed entirely. That's very strange, Angela," he continued to stare so I did the only thing I could do. I stared back.

I wondered if that was the Guardian in him that was coming out. Perhaps he didn't one hundred percent trust me after all? I didn't squirm under his dark stare, but I wanted to.

"Are you okay? Can you go on?" I couldn't deny his concern for me, I just wished I knew what he was thinking.

"Yeah, I'm okay. Let's get going."

The aisles got smaller and smaller until we were walking single file. Jody insisted I go behind him, and I was feeling too ill to argue. I looked at my feet as we walked. My purple Uggs made no sound on the burgundy carpeted floor. I hated carpets. I don't know why, but I always felt like they were hiding something. Like the floor underneath was too ugly or dirty to be seen and instead of ripping it out, it was covered up. Like a lie. *Gross.*

The end of that aisle split off in two directions, Jody went to walk towards the right side, but my feet were glued to the spot. The sign on the wall said *banos*, I knew enough Spanish to translate it. I don't know why I was so interested in the restrooms, but I just knew we had to go that way.

"Jody, this way."

"How do you know?"

"I don't know. Trust me?" If only he knew how much I meant that.

The last couple of hours had pretty much turned my life upside down. My own father hadn't trusted me enough to tell me about my real mother. My mom, or step mom as I now knew her to be, was a thief, a cheat, a liar, and apparently had no reason to stick around anymore.

My family was in shambles and I had no time to explore my feelings about any of it! Not until I got my dad out of the mess, he was in because of mo—, *because of Kailey*. I knew that I would never be able to help him if I didn't start trusting in myself first.

"Look, I can't explain it, Jody, but I just know it."

"Okay, Angela, I do trust you. I don't know why, but I do. Let's go."

5

CASTING MAGIC

The hallway to the bathroom was brightly lit. So much so that I was forced to shut my eyes for a second. When I opened them, I had to squint against the contrast between the rest of the museum and the unforgiving fluorescent lighting. Jody held one of my hands and the other rested on the cell in my pocket. I was a little attached to my iPhone, I know, but most teenagers I knew were.

I felt the smooth skin of Jody's palm under my fingers and it made me think of his other hand. The Pentangle that marked the other one would probably feel different under my fingers. I recognized that he did not hold my hand with that one because he needed it free just in case, he needed to use magic in a hurry.

I know most people think Witches just wish for

something and it happens, but that is rarely the case, if ever. Most Witches need rituals, spells, books, charms, and yes, amulets to help them cast.

You see, magic is finite. It can be elemental or blood magic, but there is only a certain amount in this or any other realm.

Witches are born with a talent for magic. Power can be given, inherited, and sometimes found by accident or retrieval in neutral zones, kind of like ship salvaging. And yes, it can even be stolen. White Witches do not steal magic, we usually inherit ours.

I know my father would never do business with a Dark Witch. He clearly didn't know about Desearo's ambitions or Kailey's for that matter. But that wasn't important now. None of it was. Whatever the reason for it, my dad's life was now forfeit if I didn't get the Naga Amulet back. Sandor Blum needed it to inherit his mother's magic. It was his right. If Desearo had it, that mean he was going to try to unlock the power for himself. That was a big no-no.

The hallway ended abruptly after the restroom door, but still I felt a pull. I looked at Jody who stared at the wall as if trying to see something I couldn't. I didn't bother looking. I tugged on his hand and walked as if there was no wall.

Turns out, there wasn't. I was able to pass through

with no problem at all. Jody followed behind me his hands outstretched like he was afraid he'd hit something.

"How did you know?"

"Not sure."

The hidden room looked as though it were carved completely out of dark marble with huge threads of gold running through it. There were no tacky carpets or cheap dim lighting. Nope, in here the whole place screamed opulence. There was a huge crystal chandelier and dozens of candles lit throughout the space though they gave off no scent or smoke. *Magic.*

There were several small showcases that held things like metal jewelry made by trolls, handcrafted iron fairy cages, dragon teeth, pegasi feathers, sea serpent venom, and mermaid scales. I knew that some creatures or beasts that were thought to be mere myths by the rest of humanity were in fact real; however, this was the first time I had seen anything like this. By the way Jody's eyes popped out of his head I could tell it was his first time too. That was not necessarily a good thing.

A huge snakeskin was coiled around the ceiling of the room. *A basilisk.* Unfurled it was easily over two hundred feet long. There was a set of wings hanging on the far-left wall encased in glass and iron, the sign read *Wings of the Matriarch Harpy of the Isle of Crete*. I swear I saw them shudder on their own.

Twelve pairs of Dr. Dre's Beatz in a variety of colors hung from a large shelf display each with its own touch screen tablet. It looked like you could choose from a select list of options for your listening pleasure. The sign on the shelf claimed that each tablet was set up with captured songs of creatures such as *sirens*, *will'o the wisps*, *wraiths*, and *banshees*. Apparently, it was possible to hear these things with no ill effects to the listener. I wondered how brave a person would have to be to try it out. The cry of a banshee was supposed to bring instant death. I don't think I would risk it.

The entire room was full of supernatural oddities. It would have taken me hours to go over each display as in depth as I would have liked. But the clock was ticking on my father and I needed to find the Naga Amulet.

I cringed inwardly at a tall glass cabinet that show-cased several pairs of Werewolf fangs hanging from an enormous headdress that claimed to be from the Celtic mythological villain Lugaid who, with tricks and deceit, murdered the "Hound of Ulster", Cuchulainn.

My best friend was a Werewolf. I was pretty sure she'd be interested and incensed by such a display. I didn't have time to study it and with great reluctance I moved on.

The room seemed to be larger than the entire museum. It was impossible, but there it was. My best explanation is that the space existed in a separate realm or reality. Like the one Jody used to store his helmets in. Not all Witches could manipulate the different planes of existence like that and certainly not on this scale. Desearo must be more powerful than I thought.

We spent more than an hour walking through the maze of magical oddities that Desearo had managed to collect. I can only assume he did that with the same manipulations he used with my stepmother. One question pounded in my brain the entire time. *How and why was dad involved with this guy?*

Finally, in the very center of it all was a huge master showcase. Surrounded by pillars cut out of the same black marble as the rest of the room, lit from within, stood shelf upon shelf of hundreds of pieces of jewelry and statuettes. I knew without a doubt this was exactly what we had been looking for.

"Jody, look," I pointed to where hundreds of necklaces bearing pendants and amulets sat under thick glass. A soft pulsating light made them appear to glow in the otherwise clean darkness of the room. The sign over the case read *Periapts*.

"Peripats? It's an old word for charms or amulets. He puts them on display just like that. The Witch has no shame," Jody gritted his teeth as he walked to the case. I understood why as I got closer.

It was as if a thousand voices were shouting from the case. *Trapped*. There was magic here and it was *trapped*! My chest hurt and my head spun. This was horrific! An atrocity! How could he?

"Let's see if the Naga Amulet is here," I spoke in a shaky voice.

My hands trembled as they hovered over the display case. I made my way from one shelf to the next searching for the amulet that bore a single silver serpent coiled around a teardrop black diamond the size of a silver dollar.

From the description that Kailey had given me, the amulet was roughly the size of a baby's fist. It should feel weird that I was no longer tempted to call her mom, but I only felt relief and, yeah, maybe a little sad too.

The chain and serpent were forged from the purest silver from Penasquito, Mexico. The rare black diamond was harvested from deep in the heart of Central Africa and cut by the first Sandor Blum in 1672. He was both master jeweler and Witch. It had remained in the Blum family for the next three hundred and forty years and had served as a conduit for the transfer of their magic from one generation to the next.

With the death of old Mrs. Blum some months ago, Sandor was due to receive his family's stores of magic according to our laws. He had been robbed or tricked out of his right by Kailey and Desearo. Imagine losing hundreds of years of your family's powers that way? *Oh man!*

Served Blum right if you asked me. I mean, Kailey didn't steal the amulet; she seduced it out of him. It was gross, but I didn't think it qualified as robbery. Sure she should be punished, in like Witches civil court if we had one. Anyway, I didn't really care about Mr. Blum except for the fact that he was an idiot who let his lust and greed for another man's wife get in the way of what was rightfully his.

I didn't even care about *Kailey's* stupid affairs. Well, I did, but only in the sense that my father was in serious danger because of them. There were tears in my eyes as I searched. *Where is it?* I could feel them spill over onto my cheeks. Hot against the chill of the room. *It has to be here. It just has to.*

"Angela, I think I found it," Jody's hand on my shoulder was comforting. I met his dark eyes with mine and followed his lead. In the far-right corner of the display was a small plaque that read *New Acquisitions*. And there it was. The Naga Amulet.

"I don't understand. Why would it be on display? He must know that Blum wants it back?"

"None of this makes sense. I know my captain will be very interested in this place. There are things on display here that are illegal, immoral, and downright dangerous. How did your dad get mixed up with this guy?"

'I don't know. He's a businessman. His gift seems to center around success and prosperity. A lot of people hire him to watch out for their investments, help them plan their businesses, and stuff like that. He even dabbles in the law."

"Hmm. That's odd."

"Well, whatever. The real question is how do we get *that* out of this case and then how do *we* get out of this museum?"

I looked at Jody then back at the case. I had been careful to avoid touching anything because I was sure it was rigged with either mechanical or magical security precautions. I closed my eyes and murmured what I later realized was my first attempt at casting magic.

"**B**lessed Be, All I see,
Make it now clear to me,
Where to tread carefully,
As I will so mote it be."

When I opened my eyes it was like a layer of glass or film had fastened itself over everything I looked at. It was strange and disconcerting. Jody stayed well behind me, and I tried to ignore his presence in the room. It was difficult, his magic was strong, and he was just so *big*, but the more I concentrated the better it got.

As I stared at the display case a sort of infrared grid appeared within it. There were pressure sensors on each and every piece inside of it, not to mention various motion sensors on the outside. *Crap!* That meant someone knew we were there. Someone had been aware of our every move. They may have even been watching us the entire time. That was so not good.

It was too late to do anything about that now. Just as I started to work out the grid in my mind a light pulsating green layer of lines settled over the red ones. This was not any normal security precaution, no, this was magic. It had been cast to work with the alarm system. I couldn't help but be impressed. After all, that was what I tried to do with my home security system. *Cool.*

"What do you see?"

"It's rather complex actually, they have a sophisticated alarm system. As if that wasn't bad enough, they cast magic over it. There are eyes on us, Jody, and they may be on their way already."

"Let me," Jody stepped forward, his casting hand raised, a cool blue light shot forth in the direction of the case.

I turned my head, I didn't want any glass to catch me in the face, but it didn't matter. His magic had no effect.

"Damn it, that's never happened before. Let me try again," he moved to step closer and I raised my hand to stop him.

"Don't bother. It won't work, you know," a slightly accented voice met us from the hidden doorway. It was him, Hector Desearo. He looked older than he had in the picture I had seen of him and my dad.

His dark hair had a little more gray, his black eyes less shine, and his stomach was a little rounder.

"But by all means, should you like to try again, young Guardian, I will not stop you. I have paid the best magic tech around to format this entire room with only the topmost security system that money *or magic* can buy," he made no move to get closer to us, and I was relieved by his distance.

"You set my father up. You made my mo—, my stepmother believe that you could give her eternal youth in exchange for something that was not rightfully hers. Why?"

"What I told Kailey was the truth, with the Naga Amulet I can in fact cast youthful beauty over aging skin for as long as the power in the amulet allows. However, I have no intention of using that power on Kailey."

"But that kind of magic isn't allowed by the white Covens, we don't steal the power of others. Certainly not for reasons as shallow as that."

"Ah, yes, your American morality is touching, but I have been casting this for many, many years."

"How many?" Jody's voice was angry but controlled. I could sense his energy, he was angry.

"Oh, going on three hundred years this spring in fact."

I could feel my brow furrow as I thought about what to do. Jody and Desearo were slinging insults back and forth. Then it hit me. I only hoped I could pull this off.

I took out my iPhone and pointed at the case with the camera app open. In a hushed voice I began my chant.

"Light bends light,
　　My will to free,
　　Unlock the curse,
Break the case,
As I will, so mote it be.
Light bends light,
Your voices plenty,
No more slavery,
Unlock the many,
As I will, so mote it be."

A red light exploded from the phone in my hand and immediately the glass from the case flew open. It landed with a crash a few inches from Desearo's feet. As he moved to block his face from the flying glass shards, Jody reached out with a lightning fast right arm, he connected with Desearo's face and the man fell to the ground. His eyes were closed.

The alarm system was blaring, and red lights flickered in and out. I fell to my knees as the echoes of magic that been kept inside the case clamored for attention. Jody rushed to my side, but I couldn't make out what he was saying. Then everything went black.

6

When I woke up, I was in the forest clearing. I heard a familiar voice and she was not happy. I felt myself smile, though my head didn't appreciate the movement.

"Listen to me, if you do not move out of my way and let me near my charge, I swear I will give you a lashing you will never forget, young Guardian!"

"No, Sherry, I like this one—"

"Ah! She is awake. Now will you please move out of my way, young *garda*!"

"Angela?" Jody rushed to my side, Sherry hot on his heels.

"Well, well, my dear, it seems you have had a very busy twenty-four hours, eh? And maybe learned something about your talents in the meantime? Ah, I see you have, but do not talk candid here. The rocks listen."

I looked at Sherry and nodded with her. I understood. She was resplendent in a dark green velvet jacket and multicolored scarf. Her hair seemed to dance around her head and shoulders in colors that varied from light blonde to dark auburn. She was beautiful as always, but her eyes were concerned for me.

"I'm okay, but Dad? Dad! Where's my Dad?" I sat up too fast and the world seemed to spin.

"Easy, easy, I got you," Jody held onto me, one arm wrapped around my back the other held my hand as I slowly stood up.

"They are bringing him now, my dear," Sherry's lightly accented voice seemed amused as she watched Jody help me walk to where a group of Witches had just come into the private clearing.

"Are you alright?" his voice tickled my ear and I squeezed his hand anxious for a look at my Dad.

"I think so," I whispered my response.

"Do you know what you have done, darling? You have discovered a virtual treasure trove of magical artifacts. The biggest in history. Desearo was able to hide the magical properties from other Witches who came to his museum," Sherry whispered as well.

"What do you mean?"

"Just what I said, child, others like your father thought they were replicas, or fakes. Only *you* seemed to realize that the items in his possession, however illegally obtained, were in fact very real. Desearo has been pillaging the world for magical artifacts for centuries. Now, we have his stores, but he did escape in the melee after you opened the case. *Brava,* darling, well done!"

I was a little confused by what Sherry was saying. *Desearo got away? Darn it!* Still, I suppose we did well. Jody and I made a good team. And best of all, Dad was going to be freed.

"Dad!" I couldn't help my cry as they walked him in. He looked even worse than before. Sherry bristled next to me.

The Tribunal entered the meeting place and I wanted to scream at the short, squat Witch in the crimson robes who stood glaring at me behind my father. Everyone was silent as the man raised his long wooden staff in the air and spoke.

"Angela Tanner, you have cleared the name of Francis Archibald Tanner. The confession is withdrawn, and all charges are dropped. The Guardian, Jody Nieves, has reported the events that led to the discovery of the Naga Amulet in the possession of the Witch and fugitive, Hector Desearo. The illegal contents of Desearo's museum have been seized and will be catalogued by a team selected by the Tribunal. You may take your leave."

"Wait a minute—" Jody put a hand on my arm as I stepped forward.

"What, it's over just like that, no apology or sorry for almost killing your innocent Dad?!"

"Miss Tanner, this Tribunal does not exist to apologize. We are the Keepers of the law, we judge, and we protect our own. We will be watching, Miss Tanner."

With that he was gone. They all were. Except for me, my Dad, Jody and Sherry. She was right beside me as we rushed to catch my father from collapsing onto the cold hard forest floor.

"Dad!"

"Oh, Frank! What have they done to you, my friend?" With a wave of her hand Sherry created a sort of pillow of air around my Dad. He sunk sideways into the invisible softness.

"Oh, Angela! You did it! Thanks, kiddo."

"Are you going to be okay?" I almost panicked as he passed out and hung limply in the air, pillowed by Sherry's magic.

"He will be fine. He needs rest and food. I have my car. I will drive you." Sherry smiled at me and nodded towards Jody who stood a little bit away from us.

I tried to smooth my hair as I walked towards him.

My Guardian. I blushed at my thoughts. He was hardly mine. But still, a girl could hope, right?

"Hey."

"Hey."

"So, I guess he will be okay, right? Your mentor seems to know her stuff."

"Yeah, she's great."

"Yeah."

"Look, I, um, I couldn't have done this without you. Thank you so much. Um, I know that you are busy and all so I won't get mad if you don't message me or anything, but if you did have the time I wanted you to know that, um, it would be cool with me, you know."

The smile on his handsome face was enough to take my breath away. He put a hand on my cheek and leaned down and pressed his lips against mine in a gentle kiss. I heard Sherry clear her throat and I giggled. Jody laughed too.

"Angela, I will definitely be in touch. Didn't I mention? I'm one of the Guardians assigned to watch over the artifacts. I will be staying in the area indefinitely and, I have Saturdays off. Maybe we can do something tomorrow?"

"Sounds good."

"Okay then. Until tomorrow."

I gave his hand a squeeze and laughed as he bit his lip and squeezed mine back. It certainly did sound like a plan.

"You ready, kiddo?"

"I'm ready, Dad. Sherry."

"Okay, just take my hand," With a nod of her head we were all transported the short distance to Sherry's car. She started up the VW bug and we were off.

It took a few minutes to get home and get Dad out of the car and into his bed. He insisted on showering first. While he did that, Sherry and I put things to rights in his bedroom. I hadn't really thought about how Dad would feel now that Kailey was gone. She just left him, us both really, just like that.

Sherry went down to the kitchen to brew some tea for Daddy while I waited for him to come out of his bathroom. When he did, he looked infinitely better. He was thinner and weaker than normal, but he was dressed in his own pajamas and his hair was washed in the same woodsy scented shampoo he favored. He opened his arms and I ran to hug him.

"Ooh, I'm sorry—"

"Listen kiddo, you have nothing to apologize for!

You saved me, Angela! And I—I am the one who needs to apologize to you."

I helped him get into his freshly made bed. Sherry and I had changed the sheets and pillowcases. It just seemed the right thing to do. Almost all evidence of Kailey was gone. Except for the divorce papers and her note. I left them on his bedside table. I figured he'd need to see them sooner rather than later.

"I am so sorry, Angela, for, for Kailey, for everything. I don't know what you must think of me, but please believe I have always had your best interest at heart."

"Why did you confess to her crime?"

"I made a promise a long time ago to your real mother that I would always protect and provide for you. In my mind, I guess I thought that meant giving you a mother and doing whatever I had to, to make sure she'd stick around. I guess I messed up, huh?"

At that moment Sherry came out of the elevator with a tray complete with teapot, saucers, crackers, and some bottles that I recognized as her healing potions.

"No, I think I understand, Dad. I'm just glad you're back and you're safe."

"Okay Frank, come on drink this," Sherry shoved spoonful after spoonful of a thick green concoction in

Dad's mouth followed by a cup of the sweet-smelling tea.

"Oh Sherry, what are you doing to me?"

"Making you better, you oaf! Now you need sleep."

"I agree with Sherry, Dad, but first, whatever happened to my real mom? Who was she?"

"Oh Angela, your real mom was something else. She was so beautiful, just like you. You have her hair and her gorgeous eyes, and her generous heart. My love, she was my love..."

His eyes closed and I looked up at Sherry. She smiled kindly at me and gave my arm a pat. We left the room together and I left a cell near his bed so he could call me if he needed anything.

"He needs to rest, darling, and I think you do too."

"Sherry? Did you know my mom?"

"Your mother? No, I had not had the pleasure, dear, but I am sure your father will tell you everything when he is rested."

"Okay. Are you going?"

"No, I'll stay in the guestroom tonight, alright?"

"Yeah, thanks."

EPILOGUE

EPILOGUE

I didn't realize how exhausted I was until after I showered and dressed for bed. I logged onto my computer as I normally did before I went to sleep and was surprised by what was waiting for me. *Pleasantly surprised.* Jody had sent me a message.

Goodnight, my lovely Fire Witch, I will see you tomorrow. Noon.

I smiled to myself as I pictured riding on the back of his Ducati with my arms wrapped tight around him. My heart pounded in my chest and

I got all kinds of excited as I thought about being with him.

I didn't even notice the flames until I tried typing a reply and the keyboard melted under my fingertips. *Ooops.*

THE END...or is it...

Liked this story? Get more books from the Grazi Kelly Universe today, starting with Wolf Moon by clicking here.

Turn the page to read an excerpt from Keeping Magic, Book Two in The Angela Tanner Files...

BLURB

Teenage Witch Angela Tanner is learning to control her powers, but it's not as easy as it looks. Especially when everything points to her being a Fire Witch. Is her awesome power a gift or a curse? That's something she must find out. At least she's not alone. She has the help of her own personal Guardian, Jody Nieves. Together, they set out on a journey to discover the truth behind her powers. Can she learn control in time to save herself?

KEEPING MAGIC

SOMETIMES THE TRUTH COMES AT A COST

Teenage Witch Angela Tanner is learning to control her powers, but it's not as easy as it looks. Especially when everything points to her being a Fire Witch.

Is her awesome power a gift or a curse? That's something she must find out. At least she's not alone. She has the help of her own personal Guardian, Jody Nieves.
Together, they set out on a journey to discover the truth behind her powers.

Can she learn control in time to save herself?

KEEPING MAGIC

THE ANGELA TANNER FILES
VOLUME 2

1

Needle-like icicles hung from the bare apple and pear trees that made up the small orchard behind our house. Mine and my dad's. Some of them were so long they almost reached the ground.

Decorative evergreens lined the back of our property. They appeared to struggle to be free of the heavy weight of the ice and snow that still held their lower limbs captive. Young green needles were starting to peak out from under the dark green patches that were all that was left of the previous year's growth.

There was no doubt in my mind that this year's wassailing would prove to be more powerful than last. More than half of our Coven showed up this year. Pretty good turn out, actually. The festivities had lasted an entire week. Corny as it might seem, I loved the spells we sang to awaken the trees.

May thy bloom and bud, may your fruit grow plenty
        Enough to fill bushels and barrels for many,
Years be they fast or time pass slow,
Bloom, buds burst forth and grow,
Wassail thy trees! Wassail!

Every day the temperature seemed to rise just a little bit higher than the last. I breathed in the scent of winter's ending. It came to me in waves of salt, water, wood, and damp earth. A witch's sense of smell was more perceptive than a human's, but not as great as other supernaturals. Still, I inhaled deeply.

A smile tugged at the corner of my mouth. After the intense cold of the past few months the smallest change was most welcome. The ground was squishy beneath my boots. Puddles dotted my backyard as mounds of snow and ice slowly melted during the day only to refreeze again at night.

It was a long, slow process, but I was overjoyed. It seemed as if we were going to experience the usual seasons in my small corner of Northern New Jersey once again. Untainted by dark powers and evil intent.

It was all thanks to Grazi Kelly, of course. *My gal, my homie, my BFF.* Okay, so I helped a little. But that's what friends do. They help each other. And Grazi just happened to be a very important player in the supernatural war that was constantly being waged between the powers of good and evil. Helping her was in everyone's best interest.

Anyway, the effects of dark magic sometimes included extreme weather. When she defeated the Scarred Sisters Coven in the woods in Bethlehem, PA, she stopped that. Okay, *we* stopped that.

It was still a little unreal to imagine I had anything to do with it. But I did. I had finally come into my talents as a Witch right before the battle. I was a bit of a late bloomer, but I finally had magic!

For the first time ever, I was really psyched for spring. Witches usually were, what with new growth and beginnings. It was a very important time for our Coven, which was primarily agriculturally based.

Personally, I tended to be more technically inclined. Maybe my excitement was because I finally had a magical talent. Maybe it was because I was sick to death of the cold. Or maybe it was because I was just so ridiculously happy.

I mean, how could I not be? It was almost Valentine's Day and I could practically feel the grass seeds beneath my feet waiting to push through the mud and make themselves known.

Oh, St. Valentine, I wonder if you ever felt this way. You married followers of Christ in secret and passed along outlawed messages between Christians during Roman times.

Were you ever anxious, excited, and scared all at once?

Balancing my beliefs between Christianity, Wicca, and Asatru was kind of tricky, but sending me to Catholic school had rubbed off on me. Dad had all sorts of reasons for it. Something about the Coven wanting to keep tabs on the goings-ons of the Church.

Witches weren't really fans of institutionalized religion, but hey, I enjoyed my many beliefs. I figured no one should have the right to tell me what or how many beliefs I was allowed to have.

At any rate, St. Valentine's Day was still few days away, but I always thought of that day as some sort of herald that spring was near. It seemed to me as if the bowels of the Earth were stirring with new life.

Though this was the month of the Snow Moon or

the Hunger Moon, I couldn't help but be happy. It was as if I could hear nature's young churning and waiting to burst forth all bright and new and lovely.

I don't know. Maybe I was being silly or just overly romantic. I mean, I finally have *one*. For the first time in my life, *I have one.*

A Valentine.

My stomach bubbled with excitement when I thought about it. A Valentine of my very own. I inhaled his minty scent and smiled. My mind had a nasty habit of running away with me.

His *anima magicae* filled my nostrils and brought me back to the present. I became aware once again of where I was and who I was with.

Jody Nieves.

My boyfriend!

Jody's dark eyes were closed as he stood next to me. His long arms were outstretched. His palms were lifted toward the sky.

His head was tilted toward the sky. Long, glossy dark curls spilled behind him. His hair was gorgeous. Thick and shiny enough to make any girl jealous.

There was no moon out tonight. No stars either. He was nearly invisible in his pitch-black pants and leather Guardian's coat. I couldn't help but stare at him. He was delicious to look at. Especially when his lips twitched as if he was trying to suppress a grin.

"*Atencion*, Angela. Come on, just ten more minutes," his voice was calm and neutral, but it sent shivers down my spine all the same.

It amazed me how he could transition from English to Spanish and never leave a trace of accent in either language of the other.

Flawless.

I closed my eyes and raised my arms, mimicking his stance, though I doubted I looked as good. Mastering my powers was more difficult than I thought. I mean, it seemed so easy when I was right in the middle of all the fighting back in December.

With Grazi.

Focus, Angela.

Okay, back to my powers. They were surprisingly strong for someone as young and inexperienced as myself. They were also a lot more difficult to control when I wasn't full of adrenaline, like when I was in mortal danger. I almost held a tiny spark of a flame in the palm of my right hand when my thoughts turned to Grazi once more.

It had been weeks since I last saw or heard from her or Ronan. The closest thing I got to receiving a message was an insta-chat post in *WolfMoon* from

SilverWolf stating that "the full moon was close and soon he'd be eating his fries with gravy."

Whatever the heck that meant. I guess thousand-year-old Werewolves weren't known for making much sense. Seriously, the dude was strange!

"Angela." Jody's tone meant he knew I wasn't paying attention. For his sake I bit my bottom lip and tried again.

Flames danced around in my head. They weren't scary or hot. Well, not to me anyway.

They grew tall inside of my mind. Full of different hues and levels of intensity. Not just orange. *No.* The flames inside of me were a rainbow of colors.

Blood red, blinding white, deep gold, bright blue, shimmery purple, neon orange, apple green, and pale, pale pink. They danced around inside of me in a melodious pattern. They rose up. Floating in the sky inside of my mind and then, they *grew*.

When I opened my eyes, my right hand was encased in a sparkling pink flame. It didn't hurt. On the contrary, it felt great. I felt great. Strong. Powerful.

Higher, I thought, and the flame grew, deepening in color as well.

Jody backed up a step. His face carefully blank.

I didn't spend too much time thinking about him just then. No, not when I held fire in my hand. The flames turned bright red and spread from my right hand to my left. I marveled at the rush I got when that happened.

More, I commanded. It raced up my arms to my elbows. And as it grew so did my zeal.

I felt amazing.

Invincible.

My breath was coming faster and faster. All I wanted was *more*.

To feel more power.

To use it.

Yeah, I could use it.

I could do anything. I was so sick of winter. So sick of the ice and snow. I'd fix it. I could make it all go away. I just needed more!

"Angela. Angela!" Jody's voice sounded far away. Like he was inside the house while I, I was in the yard surrounded by my flames.

My beautiful fire.

But that couldn't be right. He was standing right there.

I turned my head to look at him and saw only red where I knew he should be! I turned my head left and right. But all I could see was fire. I was surrounded. I panicked for a moment. I was inside the flame, true, but they were *my* flames.

They wouldn't hurt me.

Couldn't hurt me.

I was safe inside the flames. It was the only place I was truly safe. I rotated my head, but the fire was the only thing I could see. It danced and sparkled.

A thing of beauty.

It was hypnotic.

A pulsating blaze.

Warm and bright.

I wanted more, but wait... I was doing something before, wasn't I? Wasn't I looking for something, or someone?

Stay.

Dance.

Feed.

More.

Angela.

Fire Witch.

More.

Brighter.

Burn.

Burn.

BURN!

"Angela! Stop!"

Suddenly I felt cold. Cold and wet.

I turned my head. There were no more flames. No

more fire. Only Jody standing with the garden hose in his hands.

His face was pale, and he looked shaken. I looked down only to see the charred remnants of my jeans, sweater, and black leather boots sticking to my now soaking wet body.

"Oh crap! Not again." I kicked the dirt and turned around.

The walk back to the house was cold and embarrassing. I knew my face was probably as red as my hair. But surprisingly, I didn't care about that just then.

When was I going to learn control?

I heard the sounds of Jody cleaning up behind me. By now, he understood that I wouldn't be physically hurt or damaged by the flames. He knew I would need some time to pull myself together, take a shower, and change into dry clothes.

He was giving me the space to do all that while he carefully put away the hose and picked up whatever bits and pieces of my clothing were left. I wondered if I burned any of the trees. But we should have been far enough away to stop that.

Oh boy.

This whole mastering my powers business was getting pretty expensive. That was the fifth outfit I burned to bits this week alone!

Ugh.

Oh well, there was always the mall. I could probably stand to do a little shopping.

Glee!

My cheeks were still burning by the time I reached my bathroom. Thank goodness, I didn't share it with anyone. I had to get a kitchen sized garbage pail just for the amount of burnt clothing and shoes I threw away.

It was a good thing I had my own private suite of rooms in the house I shared with my Dad. I wondered for a while if I should move back into the main part of the house with him. Now that he was no longer being held by the Tribunal, and Kaylie, my stepmom, was gone, I had worried that he would feel lonely in the big place by himself.

But things had quickly returned to normal. He was busy most days with his corporation and didn't get home most nights until after nine o'clock. Besides, I really, *really* liked my own space. Dad even seemed *happy* without my fashion diva ex-stepmother around. Truth be told, I was happier too.

Finding out that we weren't blood related was probably the best thing that had ever happened to me. I no longer felt guilty for her not liking me. As a matter of fact, I thought of it as a compliment these days. I was glad she left the way she did. When I thought about how my father almost paid for her crimes, I wanted to barbecue her!

Okay, Angela, Kaylie is gone.

Dad is safe.

Deal with the mess in front of you.

I locked the door and turned to face the garbage can. I took the lid off and began peeling my burnt, wet clothes off of my chilled skin. I didn't bother inspecting them to see if anything was salvageable.

Nope, I chucked them straight into the trash can without a second glance. They were destroyed.

Oh well.

I asked once if we couldn't just magic them back to the way they were before, but Jody and Sherry both had fits.

Magic was not to be used frivolously for personal gain.

Anyway, at least I knew that my body would be fine. I mean, I was unharmed. Fire couldn't hurt me. Well, *my* fire couldn't hurt me, I wasn't so sure about regular fire.

I spied myself in the mirror and instead of turning away I faced myself. For years, Kaylie and girls like the petite and blonde, Julianna DiPaolo, and her perfect cheerleading squad made me feel like a freak with my red curls and full figure.

But not anymore.

I mean, I knew that I would never look like them. But nowadays, I didn't care. I mean, I didn't even want to try. What I had, who I was, I liked. My style and individuality. Even my freckles. LOL. There was no point in trying to look like something that I wasn't or in crying about it. I was finally just happy to be me.

And then, of course, there was Jody. He made me feel beautiful. He was kind, encouraging, and pretty freaking hot himself. Seriously, he was cover model cute. But he was more than just a face or a body. He was intelligent, funny, and supportive. I really liked him. I felt good when I was with him.

I felt good about *myself* when I was with him. It wasn't anything he said or did exactly. It was more the way I felt about myself when he looked at me with his chocolate brown eyes or held my hand inside his.

I stepped onto the blue glass tile floor of the shower stall and turned the faucet handle toward where the word hot was etched into the brushed nickel plate. A steaming spray of water came pouring out of the shower head and I stepped fully underneath it.

Lavender scented shampoo filled my nostrils as I applied it to my longish red hair. It would take two applications for me to scrub the smell of smoke out of it. I followed up with some conditioner in the same scent.

Next, I tackled the soot and ash that clung to my body. A little coconut scrub, made for me especially by Sherry, on top of my favorite natural loofah would do just the trick. I loved the subtle scent and moisturizing qualities of the scrub. She was a marvel, that Sherry.

A powerful Witch and my mentor.

There was really no one word that would describe her. She was the only Witch I knew who could claim the magical blood of several peoples. She was European, Romani, and Native American. She was descended from both Welsh and Celtic tribes. Her Romani ancestors came from both India and Eastern Europe. And she even had ties to Ancient Egyptian priestesses.

There was no doubt in my mind that Jody was already on the phone with her reporting what had happened tonight during my training.

Oh, well.

Can't win them all.

A knock sounded on the bathroom door as I towel dried my hair.

If I wasn't careful, I'd have a huge frizzy mess on top of my head. It was important to keep blotting my hair in evenly pressured strokes with a cotton towel for maximum absorption. Next came a detangling spray and wide toothed comb.

"Yeah?" I answered the knock without breaking my concentration.

If only I was this focused when it came to my magic.

I rolled my eyes at my own stupid vanity. But that didn't stop me from combing my hair till it was just right.

Now, scrunch, scrunch, scrunch, and voila.

"You alright?"

"Uh huh." I was holding the comb in my mouth and spit it out onto the counter to better answer him.

"Okay. I, uh, called Sherry. She wants us to go see her. I'll get the bike, alright?"

"Yeah, I just need a few more minutes."

"Take your time, sweet. You're sure you're alright?"

"I'm good, Jody, thanks." I smiled.

I liked it when he called me that.

Sweet.

The sound of his boots heading down the tiled stairs told me it was okay to walk into my bedroom to change. I was still getting used to being in a relation-ship with a boy. I was *so* not getting dressed in front of him!

He respected me, though. He didn't push or

anything the way some boys did. Or so I've been told. I never had much luck dating anyone at my school.

Sacred Heart Prep wasn't exactly swarming with kids wanting to date an uber-curvy redhead with an eccentric taste in accessories. But Jody, well, he was different.

He was a Witch.

And he liked me.

He told me I was gorgeous. That was certainly a first. He kissed me like all the time. And always seemed to want to hold my hand or touch my hair. It was like he needed to be in physical contact with me when we were together. A hand on my elbow or something like that. I didn't mind. Not at all. I quite liked it.

Sometimes when we touched, I swear I saw sparks. Like the coldness of his magic and the heat of mine sizzled when they met. It was like, *wow*. I mean, whoa, it was so awesome.

I applied some anti-frizz goop that I left on my dresser to my damp hair. Sherry had designed it especially for my wild red curls. I hadn't cut my hair in a few months and it was already hanging down my shoulders in soft tendrils. I kinda liked it this way. Still, I grabbed a thin, dark purple, crushed velvet headband and put it on.

Cute.

I wore a pair of heather gray leggings with a deep purple and gray sweater that was a little clingy, but I liked the way it accentuated my curves. I shrugged on a pair of knee-high rain boots to protect me from all of the mud and slush that would surely be on the road.

I got them online. They were super cute. They had this purple and teal paisley design that I just loved. I grabbed my black fully lined raincoat and headed for the stairs.

Oops.

I had to head back for my cell phone. After a momentary panic, I remembered where I put it. Snug in the inside pocket of my jacket.

Duh me.

I seemed to have developed a sort of magical relationship with my phone over the past few weeks. Like, for real. No joke. Not just in the usual teenager way. But then again, I am not the usual teenager, am I?

Actually, I could sometimes channel my magic through my cell phone. Guess I really was a techie geek. Not that I minded. If my talents hadn't turned up, I was thinking about going into software development as a profession. I still might, but first I needed to learn more about what I am. Jody called me a *Fire Witch.*

I had never heard that term before, except in fairy-tales or spooky bedtime stories for little Witches. Often the stories I heard ended with the Fire Witch being captured, enslaved, and drained of her powers.

That is, if she wasn't completely seduced by them. Oh yeah, there was the tale of the unchecked Fire Witch who would turn into a power-hungry lunatic. And then she was just hunted down and killed.

Like a rabid animal.

Some future, huh?

Oh joy, oh rapture!

Jody was obligated to tell his superiors about me. I could tell it bothered him, but what was he supposed to do? He had no choice. I did not blame him at all. He chose his path long before he met me.

A Guardian had duties. Sacred duties that he was obligated by magical contract to fulfill. He had sworn a blood oath upon his initiation.

So, what choice was there?

Besides, we couldn't handle this alone.

It was bound to come out. About a thousand people saw me all lit up like a Roman candle at the battle with the Scarred Sisters. Surely someone somewhere would have talked.

It was better that we did first. And he did ask my permission before he went to the Guardians. I gave it to him. Willingly. It was the least I could do for him after he helped me save my father.

In the meantime, Sherry and Jody worked closely with me. They were great, really. I just sort of sucked. Well, I mean, when it counted in the heat of the moment, no pun intended, I was fine. I had control. I could wield my powers with accuracy and speed.

But on an average day or setting, not so much. I was all over the place. And I was dangerous. Neither of them ever said so, but I'm not stupid. I set the back-room in Sherry's salon on fire without meaning to. It was a good thing she was a powerful Witch, otherwise the entire place would've burned to the ground.

That's why we were meeting in a clearing deep in the woods.

It was safe there.

Well, at least I thought it was.

"**A**ngela, darling, we are going to work on the *Dancing Flame* technique today." Sherry's lightly accented voice seemed to float toward me as usual.

I wondered if that was part of her magic. Her voice. It had this amazing quality as if it could make me feel calm and confident and just, I don't know, *good*. I should ask her about it. I'd have to make a mental note of that.

I truly loved my mentor. Her awesomeness was legendary. I mean, she is a real first-class Witch. Beautiful too. With hazel eyes that changed with her every thought and emotion. That was a symbol in my world of her great power.

Her reddish golden hair spilled around her shoulders in a gorgeous disarray of color and texture. She smiled at me with real warmth and affection in her eyes. We had a good relationship, she and I. I waited as she lifted her steaming owl shaped mug, filled with one of herbal teas, to her cherry red lips.

A long ivory poncho of soft wool sat on her petite shoulders. She often wore white or ivory. They complimented the many colors that made up Sherry Morgan.

"Wait a second. I thought that technique was banned, outlawed even." Jody's voice interrupted my thoughts. He spoke calmly, but I could tell he was nervous.

That was something I was just getting used to. Picking up on my boyfriend's moods and feelings. I wondered if we were forming some sort of magical bond. I had read about things like that, but they were rare and mostly just the stuff of stories.

"Yes, it was once on our list of banned practices. For a time anyway. But that was long ago. Now, it is mostly forgotten. But *I* remember it well."

"Are you sure it is legal?"

"Indeed, young Guardian. I would hardly suggest it if it were illegal."

Jody raised his dark eyebrows as if he didn't quite believe her. I just smiled. She was very good, that Sherry, at skirting the rules. I trusted her immensely.

"Though I myself do not have the talent of controlling fire, I can control this training exercise. Now, Angela daring, you have the extraordinary power to call forth and manipulate *fire* in its most basic and primal form. Your magic is naturally drawn to it. It is elemental and as with any natural force, it is dangerous when unleashed."

I focused on what Sherry was saying while she walked in a slow circle around me.

Hmm.

Without using her hands, and truth be told, without me seeing just where it was coming from, a trail of black powder fell in a thick line in the wake of her footsteps. When the two ends met there as a small, but powerful *poof.* The circle glowed a bright white before returning to its natural state.

"Black salt and ash from the bowels of a sunken volcano deep in the Pacific Ocean. Retrieved from the deep by a pod of dolphins and given to me as a gift for brokering peace with an ancient tribe of Amazonian mermaids and an old sea hag in the late 1970s," she answered my unspoken question as she inspected the circle without moving from her chosen position.

"Good. Now, we can begin. You see, this area is magicked, this place here, inside the circle shall contain your flames. And outside will be untouched. *Protected.*

The fire will not spread. That is, should we have any, shall we say, control issues." Her smile was meant to be friendly and encouraging, but I could feel droplets of sweat form on my brow despite the mid-fifties temperature. I bit my lower lip.

Oh crap.

She thinks I'll mess up.

Jody placed his hand on my shoulder. It felt good. It calmed the nerves bubbling through my veins, but only slightly. Truth was, on the inside, my stomach was churning.

I felt itchy just under my skin. My magic wanted out. I could feel it. As if it was a sentient being. A living thing bound inside of me and all it wanted was to be set free. It wanted to burn. To feed. To grow. I shuddered with the force of its need as I tried to rein it in.

I am in control.

I am in control.

"Angela, Angela, look at me. Yes, that's it. Your power is new and very strong for one so young. It is completely normal that you should find it difficult to control. And for you, more than others. Fire Witches are rare indeed. And very potent. For many years the Witch community has feared those such as you are. Feared their connection to power. Especially in its raw form. You are unique, my dear. But I can sense your fear. Do not give in to it, child. Do not allow doubt to influence you, you *are* strength—"

"But what if I can't stop it. What if—"

"No, no *what if*. You are not alone. Remember that. We will help you. Right, Jody?"

"Of course." His sincerity touched me, and I was grateful for it.

For him.

For Sherry too.

For the next two hours I stood inside the center of our protected circle. Sherry explained the flaming dance technique to me as if she were a schoolteacher and I a willing pupil.

I suppose that wasn't exactly off the mark. Sherry was a brilliant mentor. The technique was simple in theory. The main points were about meditation and focus. I was just glad I didn't have to do any actual dancing, but really, I should have known better than that.

LOL.

"The first thing you do, Angie dear, is call the fire to you. But a word of caution, if you will, in order to call *fire,* you must first understand that it is an element. A thing of nature. It does not want a master or, in this case, a mistress. Its basic purpose, its goal, is to burn, to consume, to devour and destroy. If a Witch is careless with fire it will consume her very soul. But you are a *Fire Witch*, you have the power within to make it obey you. Now, summon fire."

Other Witches used candles, matchsticks, or lighters in order to summon flame. It was not difficult, though it required skill. Still, logically, fire existed in the world and if you had a specific use or design for it, say to light a candle, a skilled Witch could cause the wick to light with nothing more than her will.

But I did not need any candles or lighters. I held absolutely nothing in my hands. I emptied my mind of everything. Pushing thoughts of Jody, my dad, school, and the itch I felt in my right boot to the back of my consciousness.

I felt power. *My power*. It always seemed to be there. Just under the surface of my skin. Pulsating and brimming. Waiting for me to call it. The fire was there too. Always.

I saw it clear as day. Now came the tricky part. I needed to learn to master it. I needed to summon it to the surface. Not too much. Just a single flame.

Small, but strong. Something I could control. I opened my eyes. Readjusting my vision to the dark woods around me took a moment. But Jody's soft gasp told me what I wanted to know without seeing anything.

The flame was there. In the palm of my right hand. I looked down at it. It was about the size of a piece of chewing gum. Not a stick of chewing gum. A *piece*. One of those little square ones.

Grow.

I thought the word and the flame obeyed. It grew to the size of a softball, feeding on nothing but my command.

Move.

And it did. Up, down, left, right.

More.

I made it multiply. Six softball sized balls of fire hovered in front of me.

This time I gasped happily. I sent them soaring through the sky one by one and then back down again.

Yes. Yes. More.

But that was the fire talking, not me.

I struggled for a moment. Six balls turned to eight.

No.

My voice sounded pathetic in my mind. Louder, Angela.

No.

I was sweating now. My damp clothes stuck to me as I battled with the hungry fire that I had called to me.

Let us out. Free us.

The Fire had a voice that seemed to be made up of

many. Like a million whispers inside my mind. Low and breathy and a little creepy.

"No!" This time I yelled aloud. I raised my hand with my cell phone in it. I focused on the power button and with one click all eight balls vanished. I put it out. The fire was gone.

"Well?" I was shaky on my feet and the smell of smoke was strong in the air around me. But the fire was out.

"What do you mean *well*? That was amazing!" Jody's enthusiasm showed in the sparkle of his warm brown eyes and the timbre of his voice. He reached for my hand as I stepped over the ring of salt and ash.

"Angela, darling, you did very well. Tell me what was going on when you tried to extinguish the flame?"

"Oh, uh, it didn't want to go. Out that is. It wanted to stay in the world, not locked away inside of me. It was like it was begging for its freedom."

"I see. Okay, well done for tonight. Think about the steps of the technique as I told them to you. But do not attempt this away from the circle, understand? Okay, then. Time to go home. You have school tomorrow." With that, Sherry whisked herself into a small willow flower and flew home on the breeze. It was really something to watch.

Jody and I held hands as we made our way to his

black matte Ducati. I seriously loved that bike. The speed and sense of freedom were awesome. Not to mention the fact that I got to wrap my arms around his hard abs and press up close against him.

He always smelled like peppermint to me. Cool and fresh. I loved it. He was silent the entire ride. I didn't even notice where he was taking me until we pulled up outside of my favorite café.

CyberSodas was an Internet café with an awesome old timey malt shop theme. They made everything from organic turkey burgers on fresh baked brioche buns with avocado mayo with a side of chili cheese fries topped with scallions and bacon, to triple-decker sundaes with organic farm fresh ice cream and a zillion toppings. They also made a killer cherry chocolate malt!

Yum.

My man knew me so well!

The place was packed as usual on a Sunday, but we managed to find an empty booth. Their clientele was mostly made up of other teens, some gamers, and a few hipsters. I took out my mini-tablet and logged into *WolfMoon* using their WI-FI while Jody perused the menu. He never ordered the same thing twice.

"So, why do you do that? We've been here like a million times?"

"Yeah, but I've only gotten through a quarter of the CyberSodas bible here. I want to try everything." His eyes grew wide as saucers as he perused the yummy goodies inside the pages of the *CyberSoda bible,* as he put it.

"You are nuts. But I like it."

"Well, thank the Goddess for that." His grin made my heart speed up.

The guy was seriously good looking.

Out of your league, freckle face.

Shut up! I yelled back at the voice of my step mom that still managed to make me feel bad about myself. Even if only inside my head.

"Got it! I'm going to have a slice of the special Portobello mushroom, scallion, and Swiss cheese quiche, a cup of Hot 'n' Steamy But Not Too Creamy Tomato Soup, and the Oh My, It's Spring Again Greens and Baby Arugula Salad, *ooh*, with pumpkin seed and craisin dressing! Ooh, yeah, and a chocolate raspberry soda! Wanna split a Java Chunky Monkey sundae for dessert?"

I had to hand it to him. The guy could order, and the Java Chunky Monkey was one bangin' sundae. I nodded and smiled as he continued to stare at the menu. I gotta say, his appetite was sorta sexy, you know?

I mean, Witches in general tended to like nature and natural things and that usually spilled over to food. It was so different from the guys at school who ate the same three things, chicken fingers, pizza, and a cheeseburger and fries every single day.

I wrote an article about the high school diet, boys vs girls, once in a foodie edition of *NewsFlash*. It was pretty well received. Damn, come to think of it, it had been weeks since I submitted even an editorial article.

Handing the reins over to my once assistant editor, Jaden Gomez, was difficult for me. But I had more important things going on in my life right now. It was that simple. But still, I got a little angry when I thought about that jerk with his greasy hair sticking up all over the place writing articles *I* would normally be writing.

He was pretentious and pompous, but if he could get over himself enough, he might really be a great writer someday.

Dang.

That kinda hurt my pride, but whatever. Not my problem.

Nowadays, I wondered if my interest in all that was a way to distract myself from not having any talents. I mean, a talentless Witch was nothing to write home about. In some ways, he or she was someone to be pitied.

Our Coven was a lot more tolerant than others. I've heard of Covens where the unmagicked were banished and worse.

"Earth to Angela." Jody touched the top of my hand and looked at me intently. *Oops*, I must have missed something he said. That was unlike me. Guess I had a lot on my mind.

"Sorry, I was just thinking."

"You often are, sweet. So what'cha thinking about now? Maybe I can help."

"I don't know. Everything. I mean, I know I have a lot to learn and need to focus on you know, my, um *witchy* things, but I kinda miss the stuff I used to do. At school, you know, with NewsFlash and my other clubs and things." My voice sort of dropped off at the end.

Like I was going to cry or something.

What the heck, Angela?

That was so unusual for me. I was not the crying type.

"I am sorry, babe. I can't imagine that the change has been easy for you. It has been my experience that most Witches discover their talents when they are children, so they haven't had time to develop other interests and hobbies besides their magic. For you, it must be difficult, huh? You've already grown into the person you *are*, with all your likes and dislikes pretty clearly identified. I hadn't thought how this must make you feel. I guess I was focused on how relieved you seemed in the beginning."

"Yeah, me too. Don't get me wrong, I am grateful and everything. I mean, thank the Goddess for my powers and all that. And I'll be fine, Jody, really. You've been great and Sherry too. I didn't mean to sound like a jerk."

"Angela, you could never sound like a jerk to me." He squeezed my hand and refused to let go. Even when the hottie waitress with cute blonde braids came to take our order. I'll admit it still made me kinda shy when he did things like that.

Like PDAs, *public displays of affection* and all that stuff. LOL. He was just so gorgeous. And he was mine.

Yikes!

"Shall I?" Jody asked the question to me without even looking at our waitress.

"Sure. You know what I want." I listened to him order and smiled as he asked for things I liked. Like my sauces on the side. And extra berries in his soda for me to steal. *LOL.*

To think that if it was a couple of months ago the

thin cute waitress would have sent my insecurities into overdrive. She was pretty. Like *really pretty*. Her body was perfect. She must be a jogger or gymnast or something. Thin and toned. And her make-up was really well applied.

This was exactly the type of girl who used to make me feel like crap about my looks. But not now. Every day, I was learning to love myself a bit more. My curves, my style, my orangey-red curls, my big lips, and hazel eyes. They were me. The package deal. And I was a pretty cool person. I didn't need to fit in anyone's idea of what I should look like or be.

A lot of my negative feelings about myself were perpetuated by the woman who I once thought was my mom. But Kailey was gone now. Finding out she wasn't my real mom was the second best thing that ever happened to me. The first was finding out I had magical talent. And maybe Jody too.

After a few minutes of joking around and talking about nothing in particular, our food arrived. We dug right in. I liked that I didn't have to hide my appetite in front of Jody.

I knew girls from school who pretended they didn't eat in front of members of the opposite sex. It was stupid, in my opinion. We all eat. I mean, *duh*. We all eat, sleep, burp, fart, pee, poop, and die. Just the same as everyone else. It's biology. And that's a different kind of magic, really, but magical just the same.

The fact that human beings crawled out of the sludge and evolved over thousands of years *is* magical. But science is science. Our bodily functions are what make us alive. Why should boys think girls don't have the same needs as they do? Stupid really. And unrealistic.

"Is it alright?"

"Yeah, it's great. My drink is a bit warm, though."

I inhaled the woodsy peppermint scent of Jody's *anima magicae* and smiled. He held his left hand over my drink, the one with the Pentacle on it, and murmured softly.

"*Inalgesco.*"

His grin was contagious, and I nodded my thanks. I took a sip of my now chilled beverage and sighed. It was perfect.

"Thanks."

The next day I had school. *Ugh.* Jody couldn't come with me. Technically, he wasn't a student. Not one who was enrolled at Sacred Heart Prep. Not that he was enrolled anywhere else, either.

I asked him about his education once. He didn't have what I would call a conventional upbringing and I was curious. Jody explained to me that he grew up in a foster home in his early years.

He attended public grammar school until fifth grade. After that he was homeschooled by the Order of the Guardians. He passed the high school equivalency test at age sixteen as was required by the state.

His talents had been discovered early, which was why he was recruited so young. He practically grew up with the Guardians. He lived with them, was taught by them, and became one of them before he could legally drive.

Little is really known about the actual practices of the Guardians, but there were ways to summon them. Tough, there was rarely a need. They seemed to know when their presence was required.

They lived in a complex known as the Fortress. The whereabouts of which were extremely secret. It was speculated in the supernatural world that the

Fortress moved of its own will to keep their secrets safe. Only a Guardian could find it.

It was my understanding that they were basically *magic cops*. Their job was to protect and guard the supernatural world. Their duties included settling disputes and enforcing laws.

Education was taken very seriously by the order. *Obviously.*

Jody was the smartest guy I knew and that was saying something. Most of the staff at my Dad's offices had advanced college degrees many from Ivy League schools. But compared to my guy, they were dopes! I guess a degree was really just a piece of paper.

Jody spoke at least three human languages and half a dozen supernatural ones. He understood complex mathematics, as I recently discovered when he helped me complete my AP Pre-calculus homework! And he was an avid reader.

His passion for all of the things in the supernatural world made him even more amazing. He had a unique way of understanding about him. And his five years as a full-fledged Guardian helped him develop a professional yet sympathetic manner when on duty.

Okay, okay. So I was smitten with the guy. Do people still use that word? Well, anyway, it fit.

Did I mention the way his dark-as-ground-espresso hair spilled onto his broad shoulders?

Or the yummy way his brown eyes turned teal when he was casting?

Mmm.

He had some serious skills with magic.

Like duh.

I guess that's why he was a Guardian.

My mind drifted around like that throughout the day. I mean, how was I going to focus on something as mundane as school when I was finally a *talented* Witch?

With a smoking hot boyfriend!

Okay, well maybe not my *boyfriend* boyfriend. I mean, he didn't ask yet or anything. But we kissed on occasion. And we held hands. And well, he was a *boy* and my *friend*.

So yeah, *boyfriend*!

"Ooof!"

I collided with something small and dropped my tablet on the pea green linoleum floor of my high school. Thank the Goddess for protective cases. *Oopsies.*

"Hey, watch where you're going!"

"Yeah, need-to-get Tanner! *Ugh*, look what you did." A frothy coffee drink sat on its side on the floor, slowly oozing out of the cracked plastic top right alongside my tablet.

Great.

It was Julianna and her clones.

Of course.

Nothing like a group of superficial, snotty cheerleaders to make this Monday any better. I looked at her for a moment and saw no trace of my best friend Grazi in her cousin's perfectly symmetrical features.

Her two clones swung their dyed locks over their shoulders in not-so coordinated imitation of Julianna. Girlfriend had bitchiness down to a science. Others could only try, but there was only one Julianna DiPaolo.

Thank God and the Goddess for that one!

"Come on, Jules. Let *her* clean it up," Lizette chimed in.

"Yeah, she's the one who did it," Jennifer said, every bit as nasty as her friend.

"Whatever, Tanner. Just stay out of my way." I met the angry baby blue eyes of SHPS's favorite cheerleader head on.

I was so not going to be a pushover for this bullying princess. She's the one who made Grazi's life a misery for so long! I figured she deserved a little of it back.

"Why don't you three just get over yourselves already? There is more to life than bleached hair and *Frappuccino's*! Clean up your own damn mess." I moved past Julianna, brushing past her arm as I grabbed my tablet off the floor and walked away.

Jerks.

I felt more than saw Julianna's eyes as they watched me leave. I was so mad my entire body was shaking. I counted to three before turning around, unsure of my own self-control.

I turned back to look at the stunned trio only once. When I did, I swear my mind was playing tricks on me.

Her eyes!

Those perfect baby blue eyes that had looked at me with scorn and disgust for years, *yup*, those very same ones, well, they were *pink*. Not blue.

Pink.

Like an albino bunny.

She blinked and shook her head. When she reopened them, they were blue again.

Uh oh.

I did not have a good feeling about this.

I rubbed the side of my arm. It was all tingly all of a sudden. And not from the polyester brown sweater vest we all wore.

Yuck.

It was the same arm that touched Julianna in the hallway. There was definitely something *magicky* going on. The residual effects I was feeling were all the proof I needed of that.

I ducked into the gym where Volleyball practice was going on. I crouched behind the bleachers so I wouldn't be seen. This was so weird. I needed some advice.

I reached for my cell phone. The screen glowed a reddish orange at my touch. This had been happening more and more lately. I haven't really had time to explore the relationship between my cell and my magic, but sooner or later it was something I needed to address.

So far, I kept my suspicions between myself and Jody. But it might be time to ask Sherry about this. As if the phone new what I wanted, my messenger app opened and Jody's name was waiting. Instead of using the keypad, I held the phone and stared at the still glowing screen. My message began typing itself exactly as I thought it.

Interesting day so far. I think I may have discovered a Witch who is just coming into her talent. Wanna meet me after school?

I had no time to marvel at this new casting method of mine. Jody's reply was instantaneous and succinct as always. After all, this was kinda like his job. I smiled at his one-word answer.

Yes.

Then the screen of my cell returned to normal and my message box was empty.

Hmm.

I checked my texts again, but there was no record of our last two texts. I shut the phone off counted to thirty and restarted it, but there was no change.

I knew I couldn't ask Jody about this. I would tell him, sure, but he wouldn't be able to provide an answer for me. He was not a fan of modern technology. Most Witches weren't.

Of course, there were always exceptions to the rule, but most of the time my kind tried to stay in the last century. Most of those in our Coven tended to be farmers, gardeners, florists, knitting store owners, nannies, teachers, librarians, homeopathic healers, acupuncturists, and so on.

The rest of the day was routine. Same old teachers, same old lessons. I barely stayed awake until the final bell rang. But when it did, I headed straight for the door. I could feel my heart begin to race inside of my chest.

I was happy school was over for the day, but that

wasn't why I rushed down the hall almost knocking over Sr. Diane, our principal!

"Watch where you are going, Ms. Tanner!"

"I'm sorry! Excuse me, Sister." I smiled my apologies, but I didn't slow down.

Jody was there. He was just a few yards away, waiting for me and only me in the school parking lot. And I couldn't wait to see him.

I opened the school doors and was momentarily blinded by the sun glistening off the still present mounds of snow. When I could finally see again, there he was! Leaning against his Ducati. His dark eyes smiling at me.

I paused, suddenly nervous. I almost forgot about my hideous uniform. It was brown and yellow, yup, the colors of our most base bodily functions.

Who designed these things?

Ew.

I straightened my shoulders and began to walk toward him. The way his lips spread in a slow smile made my heart melt a little. As if I was the only thing he saw.

It was hard for me to believe sometimes. I mean, I'm a realist. I know Jody said Fire Witches were renowned beauties and all, but I never felt like one. Other girls walked by, well, more like strutted by him and his motorcycle, but he seemed more annoyed than interested.

His eyes and mouth were hard. Until he found mine. Then he smiled. And I felt warm all over.

"Hey."

"Hello, Angela, how was your day?"

"Fine. Well, classes were a bit boring, but you know, *fine*." I never liked lying. Not even about something as mundane as how my day was. Jody's dark eyes smiled, and he tugged a lock of my hair playfully.

"Ah. Well, yeah, I guess it would be after everything you have been through these past months."

"*Sooo...*" My mind turned to mush whenever he looked at me like that. Okay, so I was pathetic, but not in a bad way. I mean, I *like* him. Seriously like him. *Romantically* and everything. I allowed myself the very real teenage girl habit of my mind going blank in his presence.

"So, where is your Witch?"

"Uh, she's right there." I pointed Julianna out to him.

She was walking with a group of cheerleaders and athletes. The typical body-beautifuls of Sacred Heart Prep. They were all talking over each other, snapping selfies with their cell phones, and LOL-ing, probably at the expense of some other less fortunate members of the student body. They seemed like the average group of mean girls and bully-jocks.

Except for her. Julianna was not participating in the usual exhibition of bad behavior. She appeared to be hanging back. Like she was, I don't know, preoccupied or something.

Not that her friends noticed. She looked perfect. As always. Maybe that was why her actions were being ignored by her besties. Her blonde streaked hair sat dutifully on her petite shoulders. Her crystal blue eyes were turned downward as if she were looking at her penny loafers and knee socks.

They were the same brown penny loafers we all wore, but for some reason they seemed way cooler on her tiny feet. I think it was the way she wore her brown cable socks. Perfectly pulled up to her smooth knees.

They never fell down or moved out of place like mine did. Sometimes twisting around and making a swirling pattern up my calves. I hated it when that happened.

Her socks wouldn't dare misbehave like that. I had to jolt myself out of my unwanted admiration for Julianna's sense of style and scrutinize her for what I knew to be true. She had magic.

But how?

And why?

At any rate, she seemed normal from this distance, if a little distracted. Then Sebastian DeLaCruz, star soccer player and all-around cutie, stopped short in his tracks. He was looking at his phone exclaiming at some UrShotz photos or some such nonsense when Julianna, in her momentary daze, bumped solidly into his back.

And then everything turned to crap.

3

An ear-piercing scream filled the air. It was like the sound a cat made when someone stepped on its tail. Only much, much louder. And it was coming from Julianna.

I watched, dumbfounded, from across the parking lot as the seemingly perfect lead cheerleader, a girl who had taunted me for years, fell to her perfectly smooth knees on the slush covered pavement. I won't say that I panicked, but I knew something was not right. The air felt charged.

I sniffed and picked up the faint scent of hyacinths and seaweed. I looked to Julianna once more from across the parking lot. Row after row of both old and new cars sat between me and the screaming cheerleader.

Some were shiny and well kept, others dented and dingy, obviously chosen by middle class suburban parents who didn't quite trust their seniors to not bang them up in the Sacred Heart Prep parking lot. Probably a good idea.

Well done, parents, well done.

Anyway, from my vantage point I saw Julianna's once clear blue eyes as they lifted toward the skies. Only now, they were glowing pink. Then, quite suddenly, rain began to fall. Cold, hard rain.

"Get on!" Jody revved his engine and in two seconds we were across the parking lot right next to where she knelt, pink eyes lifted toward the darkening skies. Her friends had all backed away.

Jennifer and Lizette sobbed loudly into each other's arms. They somehow still managed to take pictures and videos of their so-called BFF. Jody looked at me and nodded toward their phones.

I couldn't believe it. He actually wanted me to tamper with them.

Cool.

That kind of casting I seemed to have a serious knack for. One click on my own cell phone and everyone there began tapping theirs wondering aloud what had happened. None of their phones seemed to work.

Uncool, girls, very uncool.

Another click on my cell and I wiped all of their photo galleries clean.

That's what you get, I thought.

It served them right for abandoning their precious homecoming queen just like that.

"OMG! I know what's wrong, she's like having a seizure!"

Everyone was looking at Julianna as if she was a freak. I didn't know what to do. I ignored the vicious whispers that were already circulating through the crowd. Started by her so-called BFFs. I was not used to feeling sorry for those I considered my enemies. But I did. I felt a huge pang of sympathy for her.

Jody hopped off his bike and ran to her side. He placed his left hand on her forehead, effectively closing her pink eyes. Suddenly, the screaming stopped, and Julianna collapsed in his arms. I stood back, too stunned to move. He turned to me, his normally dark eyes a bright teal.

"Call Sherry." His voice was strained, and I knew he was struggling to keep her sedated.

I was dripping wet from the rain, which had stopped as suddenly as it started. All of Julianna's friends were now wailing and gasping. I picked up on their not-so-quiet whispers of suspected drug use or dieting gone wrong.

"Oooh, like, I know it must be those Brazilian diet pills!"

"Seriously? Who gave them to her?"

"No, I heard she yaks after lunch like every day!"

"Yeah, it's because of thigh gap! She's like really concerned about hers!"

"I told her she could like, talk to me and whatever, about her negative self-estimations!"

"That's self-esteem," I couldn't stop myself from auto-correcting Julianna's circle of best friends. I rolled my eyes and took my cell out of my pocket.

"Whatever, loser, just hurry up and call the pediatrics!"

"It's paramedics, now shush so I can hear." I dialed Sherry's number quickly and told her what had happened in short clipped sentences.

I didn't know who could be listening. She gave me instructions as to what to say and do. I nodded my head even though she couldn't see me and clicked *end call* on my cell.

"Okay, everyone, um, I called an ambulance and it's on the way. The EMT said to give her some space so you know, back up, or whatever." I met Jody's eyes and he nodded. He understood perfectly. Witches take care of their own.

"Oh my God, like Jules, can you hear me?" Lizette went to grab her friend's hand, but little currents of magic were still coming from her still form.

"Better not touch her just yet," magic rang throughout Jody's voice. Not a lot, but I was learning to identify when magic was being used.

"Okay. Wow, like are you a doctor or something? You are so brave." Jessica twirled her hair around her finger and sucked in a breath, which also caused her to stick her chest out more. As if she needed to with that push-up bra on! I rolled my eyes.

Whatever.

Not too long ago I might have felt insecure. I mean, I was just not anywhere near their body type. I actually *liked* food. Not to mention gaming and reading.

They liked mini-skirts and pom-poms. I didn't mind a good mini skirt. Paired with some combat boots and a plaid shirt tied at the waist, it would actually make a pretty cool outfit. But other than that, I had nothing in common with those girls.

The sound of a siren interrupted my thoughts and I turned as a white ambulance rolled into the parking lot. It hit a couple of cones on the way in.

Witches weren't known for their superior driving skills.

Anyway, I hadn't even noticed the addition of Mrs. Theodore, one of the English teachers at my school. Her cat-eyed glasses sat low on her nose as she scrunched up her face and wrung her hands.

"Oh my! I will have to call her parents!" Her lipstick stained teeth made me cringe, but before I could answer her the door to the ambulance opened.

Out popped Sherry, my mentor, in an old timey nurse's outfit. Her multi-colored hair swirled around her shoulders and her wide hazel eyes smiled as she approached us.

"No need, Mrs. Theodore." Sherry's lightly accented voice reached my ears and the tension that I hadn't even realized was there dissipated.

"Ms. DiPaolo's parents have already been contacted. They will meet us at the ER. All is well now, you may go inside." Sherry took Mrs. Theodore's hand and when she did a look of calmness spread over the teacher's face.

"In fact, all of you can go now. She will be fine." The subtle power behind Sherry's command was awesome.

The committee of vultures who had gathered to see their favorite cheerleader in a compromising position began to disperse. Some of them still tapped the sides and backs of their cell phones, which incidentally hadn't turned back on yet. Others rubbed their heads as if wondering how they came to be standing in the parking lot. And others still stood where they were in a kind of temporary stupor.

Lizette and Jennifer were a little more difficult to shake off. They were both clinging to Jody after he lifted Julianna onto the gurney. One on each arm. He looked at me, utterly helpless. I almost felt bad for him.

Almost.

I even smiled a little at his "help me" expression before walking over to claim him.

"Excuse me, we'll be leaving now."

"Wait a minute! Like, *you* know *him?*" Lizette's incredulous expression piqued my anger.

"Excuse me, ladies. Angela?" Jody shook their hands off and reached for mine in one suave movement.

It wasn't a declaration exactly, but it still sent tingles down my spine. I hopped on the back of his Ducati and put my arms around his waist after adjusting my helmet. I tried not to grin at the shocked looks the cheerleaders gave me, but I couldn't help it.

Take that, clones!

Jody drove at a safe distance behind the ambulance. We turned into the parking lot of Sherry's boutique. The sign currently read *Shear Magic*. That was funny. I guess Sherry was in a lighter mood when she chose that name.

I smiled and got off Jody's bike, handing him the helmet. He took that, plus his own, and opened what was like a little magic closet that seemed to appear whenever he needed it.

He placed his things inside of it and poof it was gone.

Like magic.

I would have to learn that spell. Imagine never having to carry around a purse!

So cool.

My scattered thoughts left my head as the back doors of the ambulance opened. Sherry pointed to the back door of her salon, the one that led to her apartment, and it opened. She snapped her fingers and Julianna's still form lifted off the gurney and floated inside the door and up the stairs.

"I'll park the van and meet you upstairs," a tall thin man with a long beak like nose spoke from the driver's side window.

I did not know who he was, but I recognized him as a Witch. He looked at me with two different colored eyes. The man held my stare for more than was polite or necessary. He tilted his head, as if trying to cast some sort of magic on me. I felt a sort of buzzing in my head, but I narrowed my eyes and then it was gone.

"Thank you, Vasco. Now, please, park it quickly. I'll need you. You two, come with me." Sherry nodded, and we followed her upstairs.

Her accent became heavier to my ears whenever she was being stern. As she was now. Whatever thought had popped into the mind of the Witch called Vasco when he had looked at me, well, Sherry must have read it.

That kinda gave me the creeps, but one thing was clear, Sherry was calling the shots. And I trusted her with my life.

Upstairs, Julianna's prone body was gently placed on a velvet covered chaise lounge. She looked as if she were asleep.

Too perfect to be real.

Like a tiny porcelain doll.

Pale ivory skin, shimmery golden hair, perfectly symmetrical features, all wrapped up in a lovely little petite frame. She was quite beautiful. Well, when she wasn't talking or rolling or her eyes. Anyway, I focused on the chaise. It was bright purple with green paisley swirls all around it.

Cool.

"Move there now, you two. Angela, Jody, each of you place a hand on her arm and close your eyes. Don't focus on anything other than Julianna. That's right. Feel the energy flowing through you into her and back again. Open lines. Communicating. Magic flows from you through her and back again like cars on a highway. That's it, that's right. Okay, *Julianna DiPaolo* what has been troubling you, little one. Julianna, *Julianna*, come home now. That's it. Open your eyes, little one."

Julianna sat up suddenly and I yelped. Jody's eyes darted to me, then back to her. Mine followed. This was not the head cheerleader I knew. This girl looked scared. Terrified even.

"I, I, I remember! *I remember.*" Her voice was frightened. She trembled violently. She gasped and wiped her face. I noticed her eyes. They were back to their usual clear blue, but now they had tiny pink flecks swirling around in them.

"Julianna, please sit up. Drink this. It's hot, be careful. Now, tell me what you remember." Sherry's lightly accented voice was soothing as it was firm. Julianna obeyed her without question. She drank the hot tea that seemed to appear out of thin air and sat up calmly. After swallowing, she wrapped her arms and hands around her legs and laid her cheek on top of her left knee. She looked about twelve.

Vulnerable and frightened.

I hated to admit it, but I felt bad for her. This powerhouse of a cheerleader who made the cast of *Mean Girls* envious of her ability to rip a teenager to shreds with one wicked look. And I felt bad for *her*.

But this wasn't the stuck-up princess who got off on torturing her cousin, my BFF, Grazi. This girl, the one who sat before me now, well, she was someone I did not know. And since I didn't know her, I didn't feel about her the way I normally would.

"She, she had no nose. *Uh*. Her, her face was missing chunks of skin. Her fingers were mostly gone. She, she made us her puppets. But I, I fought her inside of my mind. She was shocked and angry. So angry. So she, she gagged me with something black and slimy. It was gross. It choked me. I thought I was gonna die. Then Grazi came. She saved me. I'm awful to her, but she saved me. And she, she's not normal. None of you are normal!"

Her voice grew steadily louder until she shouted at the end. Her body trembled violently, to the point I was surprised she was still seated on the chaise. Julianna's eyes turned all pink and she began to levitate. A mini whirlwind formed above her head. Candles, pillows, mugs, and more started swirling around the room.

I could barely understand Jody as he shouted at Sherry for instructions on what to do. I turned to look at her, but Sherry was not where she had been standing moments before. A quick sweep of the room and I discovered her pinned underneath a massive bookshelf.

The whirlwind grew more intense. It was loud, so loud that I couldn't hear anything other than the wind. My hair flew all around my face, whipping me in my eyes and cheeks. My brown and yellow uniform was plastered to my body. I ducked out of the way of dishes and mugs.

They crashed and broke into walls and shelves. Magazines, pillows, and statuettes flew around every-where. All of the furniture began to shake and lift off the floor. Jody tried to free Sherry of the massive book-shelf, but he seemed to be having no such luck. As for me, well, I don't know why, but I walked over to Julianna.

It was as if I was compelled. My feet stopped just in front of her prone form. I raised my hand and placed it over her face. Suddenly, power surged from Julianna and flowed into me.

It was a rush, like I just drank two *Monster*s or a bucket of espresso. At any rate, the whirlwind stopped, and Julianna sank back to the chaise. Her eyes were once again blue. Though, she seemed more frightened than ever.

"What did you do? It was like you were in my head, thank God!"

"I—uh, I don't know—"

"Sleep." Sherry, finally free of her temporary prison, stood up and ran to Julianna's side.

Her one-word command hit Julianna like a ton of bricks. My mentor looked at me, her hazel eyes wide and I heard the slamming of the front door. The driver of the ambulance stood just inside; his face was a mask of rage.

———

Julianna's soft snores could be heard from Sherry's kitchen where the four of us sat. Vasco sipped from a mug that read *Coffee Makes Me A Nicer Witch* with a picture of Glinda stamped on it.

Jody was listening to Sherry speculate on what was going on with me and Julianna. As for me, I was more worried about the raven at the table.

Vasco's two-toned eyes watched me intently. I tried not to squirm. But it was near impossible. Finally, I had enough.

"Okay, that's it. Dude, like seriously, *what* is your problem?" Jody and Sherry looked shocked at my bad manners, but I was in no mood.

"I don't have a problem, but you might, *Fire Witch.*"

I tensed. So did Jody. Sherry just rolled her eyes at the taciturn man.

"Vasco, hush, you will frighten the child."

"Child? This girl has the power to burn this place to the ground with a blink of her eye and walk away from the ashes without a single singed hair!"

"Yes, well, she has no intention of doing that, do you, Angela?"

"Of course not!"

"Your kind are outlawed, feared, and rightly so! We banished the last Fire Witch two hundred years ago, Sherry! You know it to be true!"

"We will not talk of banishment at my table, Vasco!"

"You must listen, if only to protect yourself! This girl is too dangerous! For the simple reason that her appetite for power will grow. She will start killing Witches, and then what?" He stood up and slammed his mug on the table.

"No one knows exactly how a Fire Witch operates for the simple reason that the *men* who have executed them in the past were fearful and envious of their powers!" Sherry stood up too, but only to lay a hand on her guest's arm, "Now, Vasco, do not tell me you have forgotten how many Witches were executed without the benefit of a Tribunal inquiry?"

"Aye. Too many, my friend, it was too many. But *elementals*, Sherry?"

"My own mother was beheaded because she had the power to manipulate water. Have we come so far away from our roots that we have forgotten elemental power was the first to be used by our kind? Like children cowering under our covers at the thought of a Witch who can control Fire or Water or Air! Tell me, when was it that we become so fearful, Vasco?"

"When her kind thirsted for more. When they stripped Witches like me and mine of our power to cast and chant. She will not be able to control it. Her kind of *Fire* cannot be contained."

"Fire can be destructive, that is true, but it can also be a creative power. It can bring life, sustain it, save it, even. Have we fallen so far that we forgot where we come from? Have *you* forgotten, Vasco?"

"Fire can burn as well. *She* will not be able to help it, Sherry."

"She *will* too. *I* will help her."

"You will not be able to do it alone. No. She must be stopped."

"Will you help me, then?"

"Sherry, you know I would do anything for you, but—"

"Why must there be a 'but'? Have I not offered you and your Coven the benefit of the doubt in the past? Have I not aided you when there was talk of banning shapeshifting amongst our kind? I am only asking for you to just give me some time with her. She will learn to develop control. Besides, we do not know for a fact that she consumes the magic."

"Um, excuse me, but what the heck are you two talking about? Am I some kind of bad guy?"

My mind was in overdrive.

Could this be real?

Was I something that was feared and hated?

A monster of sorts?

I didn't want to steal anyone's power. I didn't know what I did to Julianna.

I just wanted to help. It was obvious to me she had power of some sort, but it was unused and uncontrolled. And, okay, it was pretty freaking cool too.

"Look, Sherry, you've got a lot of work ahead of you. You both do. I will not speak to my elders, *yet*. But soon, Sherry Morgan. I will talk to them soon."

In the blink of an eye, a raven hovered in the place where Vasco had stood moments before. He spread is coal black wings and took off through the open window.

Good riddance.

Sherry stood still as a statue. She was always on the move and to see her so silent and unmoving made my heart beat a little faster. I looked at Jody. He seemed to be deep in thought.

"Well," said Sherry, her voice a little more affected than I would have guessed, "that was not as I expected."

"What does he mean? Am I in danger? Am I *dangerous*?" Truth be told, I didn't like either of those ideas.

"No, child. Well, *yes*, in a sense, but do not worry. You have friends, in me, your father, and in Jody, and *we* will help you."

"Okay, and Grazi too, right? She can help?" My best friend was a Werewolf and a strong one. If anyone could help me, I knew she could.

"I am afraid she is not going to be able to. You see, little one, Maria Graziana has her own problems to deal with. Her own prophecy to keep. The Hounds are after her now, as are the remnants of the Scarred Sisters. In fact, *she* may need *you* in the end."

"But we defeated them." I didn't understand what Sherry meant at all. *Weren't we finished with that Coven?*

"No, child, we only delayed them. Grazi must find a way to break the curse for all Werewolves. And that will have its own retaliations, I am afraid, for as with all beings, humankind or supernatural, not all Werewolves are good. She will be betrayed by someone close to her. I have seen shadows of her future and it is troubling me. But you, Angela, *you* are what's important right now."

I couldn't argue with her there. I mean, I was only just beginning to learn what my talents were and to explore how to use them. I didn't want to lose them any time soon. I read stories about what happened when a Witch was deemed too powerful.

In the past, Covens had to police their own. Guardians oversaw, but ultimately allowed the Covens to decide the fate of the accused. If a Witch was found too strong for the good of the Coven, she or he was stripped of all powers and banished. At least, that's what I had been told. I had never seen it in my lifetime.

"Fire Witches have, indeed, always been feared and as of late, unheard of. Guardians, Keepers, and even lowly Trainers, like myself, have been warned of the uncontrollable nature of *elementals*. If Vasco does indeed speak to the elders of his clan, they will no doubt inform the Tribunal. An inquiry will be conducted."

"What will they do to me?"

"They will strip you, Angela. I will not mince words with you, I believe in being direct, as you well know. They will set up a panel to extinguish your flame."

Her words were foreign at first. Unfamiliar. As if she spoke another language. They made no sense to me at all. Then, as their meaning seeped into my brain, I collapsed on my knees. The coldness of the hardwood floor seeped through the thick opaque stockings that I wore under my brown school uniform and chilled me to the bone.

This can't be happening.

Not to me.

The Fire that I had only recently become aware of seemed to rush through my veins. It was running scared, as if it too understood the words that Sherry had spoken. Looking for an outlet for release. I closed my eyes and tried to drown out my fear.

"Angela, Angela." Jody's voice sounded frantic as he dropped down beside me. His strong hands gripped my shoulders as he gently shook me, but I was frozen in shock. Then his touch gentled. He lifted my face by my chin and his dark eyes bore into mine.

"Angela, your fire won't go out. I won't let it," Jody's whispered words sent chills down my spine.

I knew he meant it. His vow was like a spell of its own, cast into eternity and binding him to me.

My Guardian.

I fell into his arms and he held me for I don't know how long. At some point, Sherry must have left us alone. She was inside the other room checking on Julianna. Jody sat on the floor and pulled me onto his lap. I let him. Normally, I'd be concerned that I would be too heavy, but right then I had other things on my mind.

He cradled me and I rested my head on his shoulder. I wasn't sure what to do next, so I just sat there. His peppermint scent surrounding me, calming me.

Suddenly, I sat up. I had a plan.

KEEPING MAGIC

"Okay, look, I don't know what happened before. Julianna seemed to be oozing magic in some kind of uncontrollable wave. It felt frantic and unfocused, without direction or purpose. And she was scared. I felt that clearly." I paced the room as I talked. It helped me to speak out loud when I was trying to make sense of what was going on inside my head.

"Okay, so what are you saying?" Jody's voice made me jump. I almost forgot he was there, absorbed as I was in my own ramblings.

"Well, I acted out of desire to help so my motivation was pure. Now, I don't know exactly what I did, but I can feel her power inside of me. It's different somehow. It's not, I don't know, *mine,* and I can recognize that."

"Really? I thought we just absorbed power, like when we inherit it, it just blends with our own." Jody spoke with his hands on the table. He softly drummed them against the wood. The beat was soothing.

"I, uh, inherited power from my grandmother. A minor magical store, but she left it to me. Dad had me assimilate it last year. He thought it would bring on my talent. Anyway, it was from the same source as mine, so I know what you mean, Jody. I can't tell that apart from my other magic, but Julianna's is different."

"Okay, then."

"Just okay?"

"Yes, Angela, I trust you. So, what does this magic feel like to you?"

"It feels green."

"What do you mean by that?"

"Well, to me it's like magic is in color. Mine is red and gold and sometimes blue, but this, this is green. It's foreign. And when I close my eyes, I see it in its own little bubble surrounded by mine, but *different*. Separate. Un-absorbed, if that makes any sense."

"Alright, alright, uh, look, are you close to Alessio Kristos? The Romani?"

"Jody, your Guardian skills are excellent." Sherry's

voice drifted over to us from the other room. "Yes, we must get him on the phone."

"You mean Less? Yeah, he's my friend. But, um, why do we need him?"

"Call him, please, and tell him to get his grandmother on the phone." There was a determined look in Sherry's eyes that sort of caught me off guard, but I reached for my cell just the same.

"*Oookay.*"

———

"Jeez, Angela! She won't deal with her! I told you before, there is too much history between them." Less's hushed voice sounded muffled over the phone. I had to cover my ear just to hear him.

"I can't even say her name around *puri daj* or she'll whack me on the head! What's it you need?" Alessio's voice was muffled and I could barely understand him.

"Look, I don't know, Jody and Sherry spoke and then they just said to get her on the line."

"Fine." I heard muffled voices as Less spoke to his grandmother, the one and only Madame Magdelena. Romani magician, fortune teller, and matriarch of the Kristos family clan.

"Okay, Ang? *Puri Daj* wants me to tell you she will meet with you but, not, um, not the *bastard offspring of my whor-whoring grandfather?* I am so sorry, ow!"

The sound of someone slapping Less on what was probably his head made me grin. I know it was mean, but his grandmother loved him and wouldn't actually hurt him.

Sherry had told me once about the bad blood between the Kristos Clan and herself, but I didn't realize they actually *shared* blood!

"Tell Magdelena I heard her. *The whole city heard her!* I will stay here." Sherry rolled her eyes and placed her hands on her hips in an exasperated expression.

"She said fine, Less. When can I come over?"

"Skip class tomorrow. Meet us then."

"Okay. See you, then." I clicked off my cell and turned to Jody.

"We go tomorrow, then." I looked to Julianna, who was still asleep, and shook my head. Getting her home was going to suck.

This was one messed up Monday.

———

The next morning, I called school and left a message that I was too sick to go in that day. I dressed in a pair of blue jeans, a dark green blue cable knit sweater with a V-neck, and a pair of knee high, dark green leather boots. I threw on my North Face and went outside to meet Jody.

He handed me a helmet and I strapped it on over my curls. They were extra bouncy and unmanageable today. I sucked it up and stuffed it inside the helmet as I climbed on behind him.

Jody turned his head and kissed my cheek before peeling out of the driveway. I clung to him and gave him a little pinch on his waist just for that. The rascal!

The ride was smooth for most of the highway, but it slowed down significantly when we hit traffic from the morning commute. The traffic lights all seemed to turn red as we met them and stop signs sprung up everywhere.

The smell of car exhaust invaded my lungs. I didn't know how much longer I could take it. It turned out to not be very long at all. Ten minutes later, we arrived at our destination.

The entrance of the Kristos family home was in an old alley in a not-so-great section of Newark. Well, one of the many not-so-great sections of Newark.

Anyway, it was not a trip I would want to make alone. I was grateful for my company. Jody parked his matte black Ducati motorcycle just inside of the alley.

Alessio had explained that we may want to lock it up just to be safe. Jody held his pentacle marked left hand over the bike and murmured a few words and just like that it was cloaked in a protective spell. Hidden in the shadows to regular passers by.

Invisible.

He always smelled a little minty after casting and I grinned when I got a whiff. I wondered what I smelled like after I used magic. I hoped I didn't smell like matches or gasoline or something.

Ew.

He must have seen my expression because he raised an eyebrow at me in question.

"I was wondering about my *anima magicae*, if it had a scent?"

"Of course. You smell like cinnamon and spice. It's, *breathtaking.*" He gave me a quick kiss on the mouth and squeezed my hand.

It was pretty cool the way he could make me feel like I was the only person in the entire world with one touch or look. Like I was his sole focal point.

Heavy stuff.

And yet, he managed to devote part of his focus to

our whereabouts. His dark eyes swept the back of the alley and the rickety old fire escapes. This was not a nice neighborhood. It was old and beat up.

But that was Newark for you. It was founded by Puritans in 1666. Valuable for its position at the mouth of the Passaic River. Where I knew it to be a hub of sorts for businesses, Newark was also famous for many things: the cherry blossom trees in Branch Brook Park, the New Jersey Center for Performing Arts, various universities, and historic landmarks.

It was also a place with a history of violence and crime. A tough and durable city.

Unforgiving.

Unapologetic.

Capable of redemption.

"Angela?!" Alessio's voice called out from behind a pile of wooden crates that lined the cobblestone alley.

Snow was melting everywhere, and puddles marked the uneven ground. I was certainly grateful that temperatures had warmed up, but it would be an ugly parade of muddy pools of water, black slush, and a general odor of dank and wet earth as the world unfroze over the next six to eight weeks.

"Hey, Less, thanks for doing this. You remember Jody, right?"

"Wassup, bro? Yeah, okay, come on. It's this way."

He tossed back his dark curls and walked backward into the wooden door that appeared rather oddly out of the old brick wall.

Inside, the home was decorated with intricately woven rugs and lamps and fixtures made of bronze and gold. The lighting was bright. Brighter than I expected. But I guess I was being kind of rude.

I mean, what did I know about the Romani people anyway?

Silly old stories of gypsies who lived in caravans?

People who told fortunes and sold potions on the road, where they lived secret, wild lives.

In truth, it sounded kind of romantic and maybe even a little bit appealing to me. But they were just stories. And nowadays, they didn't like being called gypsies. They were Romani. And I was a Witch.

No judgments here.

We walked into the kitchen where a tall slender woman stood in front of a large butcher block. She was chopping up a mountain of dried leaves. I guessed they were herbs of some sort. She did not acknowledge us but kept to her work.

I watched in silence. There was a certain poetic beauty to the rhythmic chopping. It reminded me of Sherry when she was mixing things for me or her beauty shop clientele.

Only, Sherry used measuring spoons and cups and worked on a marble table. This woman seemed to know just how much of each dried leaf she needed. As if she were in perfect harmony with her work.

Cool.

She reached into a ceramic pot and pulled out a pinch of something or other. I couldn't tell what it was. She sprinkled it on top of the pile of finely chopped herbs. She scooped up the mixture onto a piece of paper. Then she poured it into a bronze teapot.

Next, she lifted a whistling iron kettle of boiling water and poured it on top of the mixture. The smell was pungent, but not altogether unpleasant. I looked back to the woman herself.

She was older, but I could not guess her age. She was attractive and seemed to exude an air of authority around her. Alessio stood silently by, his head lowered as if to show respect.

Her gray-streaked black hair was pinned up on the top of her head in big, sleek curls. If it was down, I imagined it would resemble Less's own black curls. She had on navy blue wool slacks, sensible flats, and an ivory and navy blouse. She wore light, tasteful make up, and only small gold earrings donned her ears.

This was definitely *her*.

The one and only Madame Magdelena.

The magic in the air was undeniable. It felt different than mine, but strong.

Very strong.

I focused for a moment on it. The second I identified her magic, I felt it pulsate and dance around her as she made her tea. Slow throbbing movements, like a waltz compared to my own burgeoning magic that sometimes felt like a mosh pit.

Finally, she turned to me. Her face unsmiling, but open and courteous just the same. She placed the teapot on the table while Alessio gathered some cups and spoons. Small bowls of sugar, honey, cream, and lemon followed.

"So you are the one I have heard much about, then? The *Fire Witch* reborn." Her voice was accented and deep. It reminded me of an old Marlene Dietrich film I had seen late one night on AMC. In fact, she rather resembled the late actress,

"Uh, I guess so." I was still uncomfortable with the idea that I was some unknown magical elemental. It was a frightening thought.

"You guess so? Child, we of the magicked folk have waited a hundred years for you. Come sit, have some tea. Then, we shall talk. And you. Guardian, protector of all creatures and keeper of the balance of good and evil, you are most welcome to my table." Madame Magdelena raised a hand in welcome and gestured toward a chair.

Jody bowed and held a chair out for me before seating himself. It was weird. I mean, I felt no threat or animosity, but at the same time the image of little modern grandma making tea did not jive with the huge amount of power I knew was there.

My own magic seemed to be racing around in my blood. I closed my eyes and I could see bright red flames flickering in my mind.

Power.

More.

Hungry.

Feed.

I opened my eyes to see Madame Magdelena peering into mine. Her own were narrowed and a smile played at the corner of her unlined mouth.

"You can hear it, can't you? Calling you to take what is not yours? Yes, I can see that you can. You have amazing willpower then, child, to resist a cache of magic as great as my own. But just so you know, Romani magic is no good to the likes of you of the Coven Reallta." She sat back in her chair.

"How do you know that?"

"You would not be the first to feel desire for our

powers. But in truth, you would not know how to control it. You would not be able to use it. Your tradition is based in healing and fertility. The production of healthy animals, crops, and herbs. My tradition is based on dreams and futures. Different magic requires different things from the different peoples of this planet. For thousands of years the northern tribes controlled the air as the southern ones did the water, and we who live in the in between, in this ungrateful and unforgiving era of time, we do what we do best, we survive." She sipped quietly, and I lifted my cup.

The tea smelled pleasant enough, though vaguely skunky. It reminded me of green tea. I added sugar and lemon and took a sip. Searing hot pain was all I felt on the tip of my tongue.

I tried to spit it out, but it slithered down my throat like a snake. It was vile.

Poison.

I am being poisoned.

That was the only thing I could think of to explain what was happening to me. The grotesque liquid burned its way down my throat.

I gripped my neck and tried to force it back up and out of my mouth. But the harder I tried, the thicker and more potent the liquid became. I could not open my mouth to spit or scream, and I wanted to do both so very badly.

I dropped the fragile cup in my panic and spilled the contents everywhere. I wasn't aware of anyone around me.

I was desperate.

I needed air.

I couldn't swallow the putrid potion.

It was killing me.

Stop.

I just wanted it to stop.

Tears spilled form my eyes. I became aware of Jody's hands on my shoulders. But there was nothing I could do. Nothing he could do.

It was all over.

My life was over.

I never expected to meet my end at the bottom of a teacup. I was sure there was a lesson there or maybe even an irony, but I couldn't find it. I simply closed my eyes.

Suddenly and without warning, the pain stopped. The thick, burning liquid dissipated and I was able to breathe again. Cool, fresh air filled my lungs. I gasped as I greedily sucked it in.

I became aware of hands on my arms and the face of my boyfriend hovering over me from my new position on the floor. I coughed and wiped the tears from my eyes.

Thank the Goddess for waterproof mascara!

Really, Angela, that's what you're thinking about.

I coughed again.

"Angela, are you alright?" Jody had his hand on my back. He helped sit me up and then pulled me to my feet. He looked terrified and more than a little concerned. But he also seemed a bit, I don't know, guilty or something.

"What the heck was that?! Jody? You knew that would happen, didn't you?" Jody ducked his head as I sat down, reaching for a napkin. I desperately wanted a glass of water, but there was no way I was asking that lady for anything to drink!

I used my napkin to wipe up the tea that spilled onto my leg. Alessio mopped up the rest of the mess. He also seemed to be aware of what his grandmother had been up to. A red blush crept up his olive toned cheeks and he couldn't meet my eyes.

The jerk!

"Good! Now I know your intentions are pure, *Fire Witch*. You have no designs on my powers. Please understand I had to test you."

"You could have just asked me!"

"Yes, well, sometimes our powers have ideas that

our minds do not. *N'cest ce pas?* The Guardian suspected I would test you, but he could not be sure how. And my grandson, well, he is *my* grandson. Your friend, to be sure, but familial loyalty is a very serious thing to me and mine." Her lightly accented voice was clear and strong.

"And if I had wanted to try and go after your powers, what then?"

"Then we would not be having this conversation, my dear."

I gulped as the meaning of what she just said finally made itself apparent to me. Had I wanted to try for the Romani's powers, I would be dead right now.

Gulp.

Madame Magdelena seemed to know exactly what I was thinking. How else could she so clearly address the thoughts running through my head? She lifted her hand and picked up a lock of my long red hair. I think I stopped breathing for a second.

Please don't pull it out!

As she rubbed the curls between her fingers, she looked me over very slowly. I bit my lip, still a little self-conscious. I mean, despite what people said about Fire Witches, I was no beauty. Her dark eyes roamed over my face and I knew that any minute I was going to start sweating.

My hair was orangey red, as were my freckles. I was a bit on the plump side, but I had zero intention of starving myself to fit in with modern day ideas of beauty. I was just beginning to really like myself, but I had no illusions of what others saw when they looked at me.

What was that about beauty being in the eye of the beholder...

After finding out that the beautiful and willowy Kailey was my stepmom, I had a newfound inner sense of peace. I was no longer some freak accident of genetics. The beast to Kailey's beauty. I no longer felt bad about my looks. If someone found my looks to be a disappointment, they could go hang for all I cared.

"You must not concern yourself with the way others see you, child. You are a gem, truly. The fire in your soul is reflected in the red curls of your hair and the smattering of glitter on your skin that you call freckles. Now, what have you really come to see me about?"

She sat back down, and I told her everything that had happened with Julianna. I wanted to ask her what else she knew about me and about Fire Witches, but it wasn't the right time. Jody and Alessio stayed there at the table. Quiet and strangely supportive. Though, if

Alessio supported me or his grandmother, I wasn't sure. Maybe both.

"A *green* magic you say? And you saw this? Hmm, that is very interesting. Tell me, has the girl come into contact with Dark magic as of late?"

"Yes. And from what I understand, her mother is from a line of Witches but has no powers herself."

"And her father is the little Hound's uncle, yes?"

"Yes. Julianna is Grazi's first cousin."

"And while that one goes off to fight the *armaya* that befell her people ages ago, this one remains untouched by magic until now?"

"If by *armaya* you mean the Curse of St. Natalis? The one that keeps Werewolves from connecting to their Wolves except for on the full moon. Then, yes. That is what Grazi is doing. She is looking for a way to break the curse." I felt a twinge of sadness.

Poor Grazi, on the run and on her own. Well, not really. She had Ronan with her and SilverWolf. But still, I wished I could help her.

"You worry about her? That is good. That means you have developed a very strong bond. Human bonds like friendship keep us from overusing our powers. Magic is above all things, seductive. Even those with the best intentions must tread carefully. That is one reason why casting is regulated so. Yes, I see by your face that you mean to ask if we Romani regulate it also. Indeed, we do. There are those who strive for too much power, too much to benefit themselves or anyone else. And that is why it is important for you to keep that human bond, Angela. It will keep your intentions pure."

"I miss her." My voice cracked a little. I didn't intend to reveal so much about myself, but this talk of Grazi was unexpected. I sniffed once and wiped my eyes before I embarrassed myself by crying.

"She is getting closer to finding a resolution. Take comfort, this I have seen in my own dreams. Now for the cousin, Julianna DiPaolo. The blood of the Benendanti runs in this one also."

"Yes, I've been researching that. Benendanti is a type of shapeshifter, right?"

"It is a little more complicated than that. Benendanti is an Italian word meaning 'good walkers', which is precisely what they were known for. They have the power to walk in dreams, like your friend Grazi. Now, she is unique for she is also Werewolf. But it is true, the Benendanti can sometimes shift into animals, most favorably birds of prey. But they are also Witches of a sort. They have magic, my dear. Secretive, though the remaining Benendanti in Northeastern Italy are, that much I have found out."

"Does Grazi know any of this about herself?"

"She knows enough for now. But my, my, it is an interesting world we live in! To have a Fire Witch and the Benendanti back among us again! It has been an age and then some."

I watched as Madame Magdelena lifted her left hand. She reached just behind her head and instantly Alessio placed a candle in it. She set it in the center of the wooden table that we were sitting around. I liked candles. I was used to them. Witches preferred candle-light to artificial light for many things, especially when channeling power. The candle was thin and tall. It's color a very plain and ordinary ivory.

"There are many *durane svatori*, superstitious tales of Fire Witches and Benendanti. Let us find some truth, instead." She looked at the candle and in a breathy voice she whispered one single word.

"*Yog.*"

5

Flame erupted from the wick of the candle at Madame Magdelena's whispered command. *Yog* was the Romani word for *fire*. I don't know how I knew this, I just did. It glowed an eerie sort of blue. Like something out of space and time.

Madame Magdelena waved her hands about in a conical pattern. Her eyes were closed, but when she opened them, they were the same otherworldly shade of blue as the flame of the ivory candle.

A strange aroma filled the room, like some kind of masala spice. It permeated the air as she tapped into whatever vein of magic this was. I shivered in my seat despite the comfortable temperatures. I had never seen such a raw display of power. And so contained.

She was truly a master.

Suddenly, she grabbed my wrist and I jumped in my seat. Jody leaned forward as if to move, but Less stopped him. Jody didn't seem pleased, but I trusted Less. He wouldn't hurt me and by extension I didn't think he'd let his grandmother hurt me either. I relaxed in her cold grip.

"I feel the power you contained from Julianna. It has not melded with yours. No, you have placed a bind on it, a temporary hold. Very advanced magic for one so young. But you have incredible power, Angela. *Very strong.* Ah, I see, your mother willed it to you. It has been contained inside of you and only now has come forward since your own life has been put in danger after danger." She whispered in a language I did not understand or recognized before continuing again in English.

"Yours is a proactive power and yet, it can be destructive at the same time. *Ancient and secret.* Kept hidden from your Coven's Tribunal. It is old, yes, thousands of years it has been in existence. But this magic has been unused for too long. *Unruled.* Yes, I see that now, you must learn *control.* Magic can have a life of its own and the *anima magicae* of a Fire Witch is truly dynamic. The Fire wants out, but it does not yet recognize you as master. It is dangerous. It has consumed before. It will again, unless you can stop it.

Your mother tried, but she failed. Her focus divided, her fears overran her control."

"What? How do you know about my mother?"

"I can see her as she was. Beautiful and young with flaming hair and a child on her hip. She could not truly accept her destiny. She denied the powers inside of her too long. They *consumed* her. She did not know enough about her heritage. She tried to keep her power secret and hidden, bound inside of her, to spare you." More whispering. I waited with barely any patience for her to continue in English again. This was the first time anyone had spoken to me about my mother.

"The Fire Witch is always female, and now I understand it is passed down from mother to daughter. With each generation a Fire Witch is born. The last three all dead. Far too young. Never fulfilling their potential."

"So wait, my mom was afraid of this power? And still she gave it to me?"

"She had no choice there. Magic like this, elemental magic, seeks its master. Your family line is an old one. The power that has passed to you is a pure vein. Magic like that was created at the beginning of time. We have simply forgotten it. But do not fear it. That way leads to disaster."

"The same disaster that befell my mother. Is that why she died?"

"Yes, child. I am sorry for your loss. Your mother was a shy one, scared, and made to fear her magic. You see, the rumors of the evil that a Fire Witch was capable of must have led her to fear herself."

"Did I steal her powers?" My question leaked out of my mouth in a childlike whisper. I was almost embarrassed, *almost*, but at this point my fear was tangible. There was no worse thing for a Witch to do. Even murder can be made right, but to steal another's power was unforgivable.

"No child, the myth of the Fire Witch magic thief has long been passed around in the supernatural community. But I have never seen this. Not in my many long years on this Earth. The intent to steal is inside of oneself. You are not bad because of your powers, and your intentions have not changed since discovering this thing about yourself. Fear feeds fear. It is more dangerous than magic and leads to more destruction than any supernatural powers I have ever witnessed. Just look at humankind and what they are capable of. No magic there, just hate and fear."

"Okay, so how do I get rid of the powers I took from Julianna? Can I give them back to her?"

"This I cannot be certain of. But when the time

comes, I believe you will know what to do. Tell me, does this girl know about her magical heritage?"

"No. I don't think so."

"Ah, I see. Well, then perhaps when you explain it all to her, she will have more insight on what she wants to do with her power."

Great, just what I wanted to do. Explain to the resident homecoming queen that she had a supernatural heritage and it was coming to life now.

By the way cheer captain, did you want your witchy powers back now?

The ones that had you screeching on the floor of the parking lot.

Oh yeah that convo was going to go over just great!

———

We left Madame Magdelena's after another thirty minutes or so of discussing the potential of my powers. I had loads of questions, but they were mostly about my mother. Madame Magdelena filled me on what she knew, but I knew where I had to go for answers. Things had been sort of tense between us. Still, it was time I faced him.

I jumped off the back of Jody's motorcycle right

outside my father's offices at Tanner Global Enterprises in Manhattan. Just on the corner of Union Square.

Jody hid his bike and helmets as I got my bearings. New York in February was cold and damp, but I still loved the city. That particular corner smelled like roasted cashews and coffee.

I smiled as I passed the street vendor who I had known since I was a little kid. I remembered afternoons with my Dad at his office. Playing on the carpeted floor with crayons and copier paper, stuff like that. We always had a good relationship, despite my difficulties with Kailey.

Jody was right on my heels as I walked into the building. The doorman didn't recognize me. I had to show him my ID before he buzzed me in. It had been too long since I had come to visit my father at work.

"Sorry, Miss Tanner!"

"No worries!"

"Shall I call your father and let him know you're coming?"

"Um, no, it's a surprise."

I headed toward the private elevator and allowed my thumbprint to be scanned. Then I punched in the numbered security code, same numbers as the one in my house, but in a different sequence. *26, 14, 18, 15, and 13.* I whispered the protection spell cast to keep out magical intruders.

"East, West, North, and South,

The coast is clear, friend, no fear,

I bid you open with my mouth,

I come with good intentions here,

All is well, truthfully,

As I will, so mote it be."

And then, we were on our way. Up to the Penthouse suite where my father, Francis Archibald Tanner, founder and CEO of TGE, would be hard at work.

I bit my lip during the elevator ride. It was strange for me. I had never been nervous about seeing my dad before. I mean, he was my *dad*. Always loving. Always kind and patient. Maybe a trifle preoccupied, but he did his best for me. At least, I thought he did.

At any rate, our relationship seemed a bit strained the past few weeks. Seeing him trussed up like a turkey at the hands of the Tribunal for a crime he didn't commit was something I wasn't sure I'd ever forget. He apologized for everything and yes, he even explained that he was trying to do right by me by re-marrying that empty headed viper and passing her off as my mother.

Speaking of that one.

We haven't heard from Kaylie in months. I imagine she's still on the run. Her crimes have thus far gone unpunished since my dad would no longer be taking the blame for her actions. Though truth be told, she was way too empty headed to have pulled everything off by herself. It was Hector Desearo who master-minded the whole theft of the Naga Amulet from the relationship-challenged Sandor Blum.

Anyway, long story short, I managed to clear his name with a bit of help from Jody. But we had yet to do something that I've been wanting to do since the day Sherry, Jody, and I brought Daddy home from the clearing in the woods where the Tribunal held his trial. We had yet to discuss my actual mother.

The elevator dinged and the door opened. It was a little bit too soon for me. I stepped off with Jody right behind me and stared at the carved mahogany door that had the words *Francis A. Tanner, CEO* inscribed in gold on it. No doubt he knew I was there, but still I waited.

Jody's quiet presence was comforting. He didn't say a word, just stood by me. In the weeks that had passed since we met, I had really come to rely on him. He was sweet, patient, and protective of me.

I kind of liked that. But the best thing was the way he looked at me. Like he couldn't get enough of me. It was the first time ever that a boy looked at me like that.

It wasn't just hot and heavy teenage hormones between us. We liked a lot of the same things. Food, movies, facts, mystery novels, music, and crossword puzzles. And we were always willing to try something the other one liked.

For example, he took me on a little hike the other day and, to my surprise, I liked it. We sat by a stream and had a picnic. Sure, it was still a little cold, but he built a fire and it was actually quite nice. So were the moonlight kisses.

Anyway...

I helped him create a *WolfMoon* avatar. He chose an officer with Witch powers. A little bit too realistic for me, but I tried not to judge. I mean, it was a fake Avatar, but he was too uncomfortable to try out another magical being.

I named him *DetectiveAndy* because of my love of all things *Charmed*. You know, the TV show about three Witch sisters. Surprisingly, they got a lot of stuff about Witches correct. I suspect a real Witch collaborated with the writers, but that hasn't been confirmed.

Suddenly, a voice interrupted my thoughts. It was my father's voice spoken through the intercom. I smiled even as my heart began to pound.

"Angela, please come inside my office before you start growing roots out there. And bring Jody too."

I opened the door and saw my dad sitting at his desk. It was the same as always. Big and polished, meant to look imposing and impressive to others in the business world. He sat in his tailored suit with his jacket hanging on the rack behind him. His glossy black hair was perfectly in place as he stared at the screen of his desktop monitor.

He finished whatever he was typing and focused on me. His dark eyes seemed to smile, and I paused a beat. Unsure of myself in front of him for the first time since I was just a little girl and I had dumped ten bottles of bubble bath into the new in-ground pool we had just installed in our house. He had laughed back then. I wondered what his reaction would be now.

"Dad?"

"Well, don't just stand there, come on in. Angela, Jody? How are you two doing today? And, uh, shouldn't you still be in school?"

"Uh..." I forgot about that. I gulped while Jody addressed my father.

"Fine, sir. Thank you." Jody's response was respectful and from what I could tell sincere. But I did not feel fine. I felt anxious.

"Dad, um, I need to talk to you. About mom."

"Kaylie? Why has she contacted you or—"

"No, Dad. Not Kaylie. *Mom*. My real mom."

"Oh." With that one word, he pushed away from his desk and motioned for us to join him at the small sectional couch that lined one wall of his office. There was a round coffee table and a little intercom sitting on top of it. He pushed the button.

"Carol? Can you please send in a tray of coffee and hold my calls, okay?"

"Yes, sir." Carol's voice rang clearly over the intercom. She had been my dad's secretary for years now.

At least ten. She was close to his age. Plain looking, but dependable, highly intelligent, and always very kind. She was forever reminding him to eat and take breaks and she always, always, always had nice things to say to me.

"Okay, now I know that I have kept secrets from you, sweetheart. But don't you think this is something we should discuss in private?"

"No. I want Jody here."

"Mr. Tanner, I am not here as a Guardian. I am here as Angela's friend. I promise you that anything said here will stay here. Her safety is the most important thing to me." Jody met my father's stare head on.

"I am glad to hear you say that, Jody, but forgive me if I am skeptical. You see, my daughter's safety has been the most important thing to me since she was conceived."

"Yes, sir. And mine since I met her."

I didn't fully understand the testosterone fueled war that was waging between my father and my boyfriend. Whatever it was, they needed to get over it, so we could get on with it.

"Easy there, guys. Look, Dad, I need to find out about my mother. I know that I have inherited her magic and for some reason it was dormant until now. But I need to know more about being a *Fire*—" I am not sure which one stopped me from continuing, my father's raised hand or the brisk knock at the door.

"Mr. Tanner, here is your coffee. Hello there, Miss Angela! How are you my dear?"

"Great, Carol. Thanks. These look wonderful." I smiled as she placed the tray of coffee and pastries down on the table. She looked over to my dad and adjusted her glasses before speaking.

"Mr. Tanner, the ambassador for the *Union* has called to reschedule their appointment again. This time, he insists that the meeting take place at two AM during the lunar eclipse."

"Which Union?"

"Oh, uh..." She looked from my dad to us and

back again. He waved a hand indicating it was okay as he sipped his black coffee.

"Oh, okay then. Uh, the Holiday Elves Union. They want to discuss their plans to strike if their wages are not increased by next holiday season. The man in charge is being represented by the Howard Group."

"Ah, my nemesis! Nothing like a good battle with Dean Howard! Just mark it on my calendar."

"Yes, sir." She nodded and left the room, already recording the change in her tablet. When the door closed, my father's congenial face was gone. Replaced by one full of worry and conflict.

"I guess I can't delay this any longer."

6

My father's entire demeanor changed right before my eyes. In fact, I hardly recognized him. I mean, nothing ever shook my dad. That was the main reason why he was so successful. But something was definitely wrong.

Was that sweat on his forehead?

He coughed into his hand and reached for a napkin with shaking hands. The man in front of me was not the impeccably dressed sharp-as-a-tack professional whom I usually encountered at the offices of Tanner Global Enterprises.

Nor was he the sweet and doting father that I grew up with. The one who kissed away my boo-boos, told me bedtime stories, and made everything wonderful again.

This man looked like he was in shock. Like an accident victim. As if he never expected to have this discussion.

He seemed worried. And that was worse than the shock. He inhaled a deep breath, as if preparing himself for what would come next.

I held my sweaty hands together in my lap and tried to calm the slowly increasing pounding inside of my chest.

What could he possibly have to tell me that I didn't already know?

I knew all about the woman he used to be married to, the one and only Kaylie, who was, thankfully, not my biological mother. I can't even begin to count the times I've exclaimed "*thank the Goddess!*" to myself over that little gem of information.

I knew I was almost definitely a Fire Witch. And I knew he wasn't infallible. Something all children find out about their parents, eventually.

So what could be so bad as to cause that particular mixture of fear, shock, and grief in his eyes?

What could make my unshakeable powerhouse of a father turn pale and shaky?

What secrets were left between us?

I understood that what he did, he did out of love for me. His only daughter. And I forgave him for all of it the moment he was cleared by the Tribunal and I was able to bring him home. My father was a good man, a talented Witch, and a loving dad.

So what was he so nervous about?

We sat in uncomfortable silence until, finally, he raised his head and looked directly at me. His dark brown eyes were full of turmoil. I braced myself.

"Angela, first, let me say that as your father my first job since the second you were born has been to protect you. Always."

"I know that, Daddy."

"Your mother was a very special woman. I loved her the moment I laid eyes on her. There wasn't anything I wouldn't have done for her."

"Okay—"

"Please, sweetheart, don't interrupt. I, uh, am having a difficult time here, and I know I deserve it, I've made mistakes, but it's time you knew the entire truth."

I clasped my hands together as he continued to speak. Jody's presence was in the back of my mind, a solid rock of support. I needed it just then.

"Here, take a look at this." He took a folded piece of paper out of his wallet and handed it to me.

It was a photograph. There was a crease right down the center. It was soft and worn, as if he looked at it often. The edges were faded too. I imagined that was from where he held it. I admit, I hesitated. I was afraid to open it.

"Go on, then. Have a look."

His gentle tone soothed the nerves that had begun to run amok in my stomach. Somehow, after looking from him to Jody and seeing their support and more, much more, I gained the courage to unfold the photo.

Inside, a pair of warm hazel eyes looked up at me. The woman in the picture was laughing, a chubby baby with orange fuzz for hair and dressed in a bright pink ruffled dress was smiling in her arms. Red curls, much like the way mine looked now, spilled down the woman's back.

She had a smattering of freckles across the bridge of her slightly upturned nose. Her pale skin glowed in the sunlight. But not as much as her smile did.

She had a special radiance about her. A warm glow of love and happiness that made me reach out and trace my finger across her face. She was in a word, *beautiful*.

I didn't realize I was crying until Jody handed me a tissue. I wiped my face and looked up to meet the dark glistening eyes of my father. I guess the memories were strong for him too.

"That picture was taken when you were just shy of

a year old. Uh, your mom, oh, she loved you so much. She was so proud of you. *Kissed by flames*, that's what she said."

"She did?"

"Oh, sweetheart, of course she did. You were everything to her."

I can't even begin to describe how I felt after hearing that my own mother, versus the woman I grew up with, had loved me once. That I was lovable. I was trembling all over with the knowledge. My heart felt heavy and light all at the same time.

"I don't know what to say."

"You don't have to say anything. She was your mother, and I am sorry I denied you knowledge of her for so long—"

"Um, Dad?"

"Yeah?"

"What was her name?"

My voice sounded muffled, nothing more than a whisper. Jody's strong hand cupped my shoulder and I welcomed the weight of it. This was the biggest moment of my life to date. I was glad he was there.

Dad bowed his head. A single tear spilled from his eye. I reached over the coffee table and took his hand in mine. My heart was racing inside of me.

Acid bubbled up from my stomach, I felt as

though I would be sick. This was the closest I had ever come to knowing my real mother. The feeling was unlike anything I had ever experienced.

"I never told you that, did I? I am so sorry. Um, her name was *Caitlin Anne Alison*."

"Caitlin Anne Alison."

"Yeah, but I called her Catie."

"*Catie*. I like that."

"She said you were her special little angel, that's why we named you Angela. Oh, *by the Goddess*, she was so beautiful. Just like you. She knew you would be blessed." He squeezed my hand before continuing. "You know; you have a famous ancestor. A Witch from your mother's side of the family."

"I do?" I looked from my dad to Jody. He had been quietly listening to everything with a certain respectful detachment, but he perked up at this bit of info. I smiled and turned back to my father. Jody loved anything that had to do with the history of magic.

"Yes, you do. You see, about seven hundred years ago your ancestors lived in Northern Ireland. That's where your mother's people are from."

"I always wondered how I could have all this red hair and not be Irish." I shook my head and remembered my second grade family tree and putting down my father's German and Kaylie's Swedish flags.

Hmm. Go figure.

"Have you ever heard of Dame Alice? Alice Kyteler?"

"No. I never heard of her."

"You, Jody?"

"I recall some vague information about her in our records."

"Well, she was a famous Witch. She was accused by normals in her village of poisoning her husbands. She had four of them, which at that time wasn't necessarily unusual. Life was hard back then." He took a sip of coffee and began again.

"Anyway, she was accused of murder and of denouncing Christ in doing so. They believed she used magic to kill all of them. So she was arrested. They decided to try her for Witchcraft, which was common enough during that time period. Unfortunately, or fortunately, depending on how you look at it, mostly *normals* were accused and hung."

"Ew, dad, that was terrible for anyone! A lot of innocent women died."

"I know, I know. It was fascinating to study all the Witch trials when I was in law school. Well, anyway, in this instance an actual Witch was arrested, but Dame Alice escaped. It's become something of a local legend in that part of Ireland. What the normals don't know is how or where she escaped to, so it is still an unsolved mystery over there."

"Let me guess, she went to the *New World*?"

"Actually, she didn't. She went south. Into England. She settled in a small section of London. Alice set up shop selling herbs and cure-alls. She healed people in secret. Of course, she had to move about every twenty years or so since she did not age like the normals around her."

"She didn't?"

"Nope. Surely you know the tales. Some Witches are able to stretch their lifespan many, many years."

"I thought that was just a myth?"

"It's not," Jody's quiet answer only led me to think up more questions.

Who? How? When? Why?

But I quieted my mind and listened instead. The journalist in me understood that now was not the time for me to go off on a tangent asking irrelevant questions.

"No, it's not. And Alice lived that way for roughly two hundred years. Moving about the countryside. Taking different names. *Then,* she caught a ship to the new world, reverted back to her original name, Alice Kyteler, and settled here in around 1550. In what would eventually be New Jersey."

"Wow." I couldn't help myself. What an incredible tale! Jody seemed interested too. He sat quietly listening to every word my father spoke. I guess a Guardian would find this a bit interesting.

"Yeah, *wow*. But that's not all. You see, at the time normals were hunting Witches everywhere. A lot of us fled and came to the New World in hope of building a more tolerant landscape. Alice soon fell in love with such a Witch. John Fox was his name. He wanted to protect his kind in a world of fierce religious rule. He started brokering meetings between Covens. His vision was to have one Coven to unite them all."

"Yes, that's true. I've read about past attempts to control groups of Covens of Witches throughout history. John Fox was not the first to try," Jody's voice rang with anger.

It was a strong belief of his that no one person had the right to rule over any group of peoples. And a dictator in control of that much magic would be unstoppable. It was not something he took lightly as Guardian. I have to say, I agreed with him.

"No, he was not. At any rate, Alice shied away from his political ambitions."

"She kept to their home and land. Never one to participate in rituals held sacred by the Covens. She kept her age and her history secret,"

"Life was pretty ordinary at that time. A few years later she gave birth to two children. Twins. One died at childbirth, but the other, a boy, well, he survived."

"Her husband's political ambitions diminished as he grew older. Still, he remained very respectable in the community. Alice herself was treated very well by her peers because of this."

"Then, there was an outbreak of disease, a plague. John caught the disease and was among the first to die. A few of the local Witches questioned Alice, jealous of her apparent youth and beauty. Alice went to work mixing some of her famous healing potions."

"But even she didn't know about vaccinations back then. Her son soon became ill. And Alice, well, she worked tirelessly to save him. And because he showed no signs of any magical ability, that made his life all the more precious to her."

"What did she do?"

"This is the part of the tale Catie told best. I don't have her fervor, but I hope I can do it justice. After a particularly long night helping the sick and mixing tonics, Alice visited her son's bed last. She changed the linens, fed him a clear broth, and gave him her most potent mixture of herbs and spells,"

"Completely depleted of all her energy, she began her nightly vigil. She sat down in a half-broken cushion-less chair as close as she could get to the still and silent form of her young son. The other women of the town, some of them Witches, also spent time at the newly built Church that had become a makeshift hospital. A young Witch whose name has since been forgotten was one of those there that night." My father shifted in his seat. I could tell he was physically uncomfortable, but he was also really getting into his tale. And so was I.

"Whether it was her father or brother or even husband who had died from the plague, it is no longer remembered. Only that she had suffered loss at its hands and had come to the Church because she too had heard the rumors about Alice. It's probable that she blamed Alice for the death of her loved one. So she put on her sweetest face and sat next to the anxious and exhausted Alice. She thanked her for her work in tending for those who were afflicted. She even lamented that she had loved ones who were not saved, *the work of the Lord*', she said. Then, she begged Alice to go home and rest so that she might try to help others again tomorrow. Alice was not easily swayed, but after some time she relented. A good rest was what she needed. So she went home. Some time during the night, Alice woke from her bed in a terrible fright. She was soaked with the sweat of a restless sleep. The smell of smoke and soot drifted in through the open windows, but Alice's mind was still foggy with sleep, so she dismissed it. She tried to quiet her mind and once again went to bed. Some time later, the town's alarm bells rang throughout the square. The smell of something burning invaded her nostrils, to her shock and horror, it was the hospital that was aflame. Her first thoughts were of her son, who was inside, trapped. Alice ran to the square in nothing, but her night shift. Her red hair cascaded down her back as barefoot she tried to enter the hospital. The town's men held her back, they told her it was a lost cause. She fell to her knees and, in plain sight of the entire town, she began to cast. A very old spell. One to find the exact location of her boy, her only relative, her flesh and blood.

"She cast a *blood locator* spell. That is difficult magic." Jody's question was low, but at my father's nod I suspected he was correct.

"Then she did the unthinkable, even for Witches. She stood up from her position in the square, the frightened townspeople backed away from her. They could have excused her casting as the ramblings of a broken mind, but when they saw her eyes, red as blood, they knew she had been taken by the devil himself. Or so they said. The Witches in the square were horrified that she would reveal their secrets, so they watched her, ready to pounce should she call them out, but she had only one focus. Her boy. She walked toward the doors, the same ones she was turned away from before, only this time the men scattered at the sight of her. I can only imagine what she looked like, fierce, determined, and powerful-"

"*Beautiful.*" Jody's interruption made my cheeks burn with embarrassment. The way he was looking at me as if he could see things that weren't there! And in front of my dad. My father narrowed his dark eyes at Jody, then he exhaled.

"Yes, beautiful. I imagine she was very beautiful. Then, Alice walked through the twelve-foot high flames into the burning building. Just inside the rubble, she found the sweet-faced Witch, her body blackened by smoke and half-burnt. She was still and unmoving under a fallen beam that was still burning, *dead*. Alice stepped past the Witch, the cause of all the bloodshed, as if she meant nothing to her. She used the locator spell she cast and found her boy. After finding them both trapped, Alice used her magic to make an escape route. She sent flames to the far wall on that side of the church. The intense heat caused the wall to collapse. That opening allowed the otherwise unsuccessful rescuers to douse the flames and move those patients who survived the fire outside. No one touched Alice as she lifted her boy from his bed and walked out of the burning building with him in her arms, all the way to her home."

"So, she rescued him?"

"Yes, Angela, she did. But people were scared. Witches were scared. Then they started pointing fingers. Who was to blame for the evil that had come to their little town? Well, Alice was blamed. She was captured. Tried and hanged for Witchcraft and because she was a Fire Witch, or a Flame Walker, they did not burn her. Instead, they had her drawn and quartered, afterward her limbs were gathered, and she was buried at sea."

"*A watery grave, for a fiery witch*, I read that about her once, but this is the first time I heard the entire tale." Jody bowed his head. I was appalled.

Poor Alice!

"Oh my *God and Goddess*! That is terrible!"

"I agree. But at least they allowed her son to live. He was not seen as a threat, being mortal and all."

"But if this is my ancestor, how did I get my powers?"

"Your mother told me that the powers of a Fire Witch run through the blood, but she believed they would only appear in females of the line, Angela. Your mother was a very talented Witch, but she, like those in your line before her, kept her powers secret."

This time it was guilt that caused my blush. I hadn't exactly been concerned with keeping any of my magic secret.

Oops.

"I take it, it's too late to hide your talents. You've been helping the Werewolves. You helped *me*. I am so sorry you had to be put in this position. I am your father and I was supposed to protect you. I made a vow to Catie that I would always protect you. I need you to know that I am doing everything I can to keep you safe."

"What do you mean?"

"I've been searching through Coven doctrine and law to find something to protect you. But you must try and keep your magic under control. Or the Tribunal will try and strip it from you. Like they did with your mother. She was afraid of her power. You see, it had been so long since a woman from your line freely used her powers that their methods of control had been lost. Catie didn't know if she could trust herself."

"Then why didn't she just let the Tribunal have them?"

"I asked her the same thing once. Near the end of our time together. If I knew that was the last time I was going to see her, I would have tried to convince her to hand them over, but she always said that her powers were not for the likes of man."

"That's sexist." My comment sounded inane to my ears, but he smiled.

"Angela, your mother tried to bind her powers, to hide them from the world, but they grew. They scared her. She told me that she wasn't sure if she could trust herself not to give into them. She was trying desperately to find a way to keep them hidden, but she was discovered and someone high up in the supernatural world found out. This person wanted them. Still wants them. She was adamant that no one but a Fire Witch of the line of Dame Alice would ever be able to control her magic. She died preserving her magic so that it would pass on to *you*."

"That tale is kind of a legend with my order. A mysterious Witch with secret powers so great and dangerous. She was wanted for many years, hunted, but she hid herself well. And she got away. Guardians have been searching for that rumored Fire Witch for the last thirty years. And it was your mom?!"

"Yes. It was. And now you know, Jody, so tell me, who has your first loyalty? The Guardians? Or Angela?"

I cringed at the question. Our relationship was way

too new for my dad to put that kind of pressure on Jody! I mean, *whatever*, Jody was the one who told me what I was first. I knew he had my back. But I wouldn't blame him for choosing his order. Being a Guardian was sort of a lifetime thing.

Still, I exhaled a breath I didn't even know I was holding when his answer came almost immediately. He spoke with a determined look in his eye and one hundred percent certainty in his voice.

Whoa!

"Angela. Always, Angela."

"Good."

"I think I can help you, sir. You see, nowadays the Guardians don't go for beheadings or hangings. We don't work for any one Coven. We are no longer guard dogs and henchmen. We are autonomous. We do work to benefit and promote the safety of all magic, serving all manner of Clans, Covens, Packs, Families, and Tribes." His tone was all businesslike, but that only made it easier for me to follow. My heart was still racing from his declaration.

Angela. Always, Angela...

"Yes, but the Tribunal—"

"The Tribunal attends to the Covens of North America only. In the greater scheme of things, their authority is severely limited. Judgments and settlements outside their realm fall to *us* to handle. The Order of the Guardians is recognized by *all* manner of supernatural beings as we employ all manner of said beings. And yet, we still take in work from the Tribunal and the countless other similar organizations."

"Really? So how does that work?" I grimaced at my own question. I sounded like a complete idiot, but I clearly needed an education in the inner workings of the supernatural world. I mean, *I thought* the Tribunal was the end all. But apparently, *and thankfully*, it was not.

"Okay, let's say, for example only, that the Tribunal sends us a notice of a rogue Witch with dangerous powers. It's up to us to find the Witch, but because he or she is within *their* realm of authority, they decide what will happen."

"Meaning?"

"Meaning *they* decide if the Witch is misusing his/her magic and then *they* take the evidence and decide the punishment or next course of action. Anything or anyone who is found guilty and is outside their jurisdiction, well, we make the decision what happens next. Sometimes, lately more often than not, the Tribunal has kept their judgments secret. Only after the fact, have we discovered that, lately, their favorite sanction has been to strip the accused Witch of his or her powers.”

“Whoa! Really? Isn’t that like, harsh?” I cringed at the thought of having my powers stripped away from me.

What could a Witch do that was so bad as to sanction that course of action?

It was beyond cruel. Like chopping off the hands of thieves.

“Way harsh. And what’s worse is, no one has ever questioned why or just where the powers were going. Until now.”

“Now, you two have hit the nail on the head. Excellent summation, Jody. If you ever decide to go into law, let me know.” My father smiled his thousand-watt smile and I slowly exhaled. The excitement of all this talk had him acting like his old self.

Thank the Goddess!

“Now, what I intend to find out is this: Who exactly is it that orders the stripping of a Witch’s powers? Which member of the Tribunal? And most importantly, *where* is the magic? Who is keeping it?”

“Desearo.” The name fell from my lips in the same moment that I realized, with no small amount of horror, that this same Witch, who hoarded priceless stores of magic, amulets, and supernatural relics and artifacts, was again stealing magic! And by any means he could get it!

But why?

For what purpose?

Surely not greed alone.

"He must have someone on the inside! A Guardian or Keeper? Maybe that little turd from the Tribunal!" I raised my voice as my mind began to race with all sorts of supernatural conspiracy theories.

"All good theories but, Angela, you must stay out of this. *Please.* Let me handle it. I am a lawyer, among other things. Coven law is my field of expertise. If Desearo is behind this I need proof and evidence and I will get it. Okay?"

"But what if I'm next on their list?!"

"I will protect you. And so will Jody! Right?"

"Of course, I will. Angela, it's best if you let your father and the Guardians investigate this thing—"

"Are you for real? You can't expect me to just sit here and do nothing!" I wanted to scream. I wanted to throw things across the room. I was acting like a two year old, but so what?

Who did these two think they were?

Since when were they all macho best buds.

Me man, you girl, sit back while I do hard work.

Oh, what BS!

Like I need guys protecting me!

WTH?

"Not nothing, no, you can help. I will bring home books for you to go through at home..."

I just nodded at my dad as he droned on. He was clearly too concerned for my safety to understand that I was completely enraged by the anti-feminine tirade he just spewed up.

As if I would ever agree to anything like that!

Whatever.

If Desearo was behind this, I would find him. He wasn't getting away with it. Not this time!

"It's the 21st Century, Daddy! I don't need protection. I need information."

"Honey, I know you think you can handle this, but Desearo means business. I will stop him. I have friends who can help. And with the proof you two got against him last year, I know I can find a way to connect him to this. If he is behind all of the missing stores of magic, this will be the biggest case of treachery we Witches have had in hundreds of years."

"Yeah, right, I get it, but—"

"Thank you, dear. Now, Jody, can I speak to you a second?"

"Sure, Mr. Tanner."

While Jody and my father exchanged contact information and discussed their next move, I stood up and took a turn about the room. I may not be working on NewsFlash anymore, but I'd been journalist and editor of the online high school rag for way too long. My mind just wouldn't stop churning. I needed order from the chaos of information that was swimming around in my brain.

Okay, so what did I know?

Well, for one, Hector Desearo was a certifiable madman.

He was also a liar.

A thief.

A criminal.

And a traitor to Witches.

He illegally kept huge stores of magic captive in ancestral amulets and other items, not to mention various illegal supernatural artifacts. He had put them on display, like a child showing off his best toys, in a secret magicked room under the guise of a Spanish Heritage Museum smack in the middle of Morristown. Right under the nose of the Tribunal, whose headquarters were also, coincidentally, in Morristown.

Jody and I discovered the paraphernalia only months ago and were responsible for it being confiscated by the Tribunal. It would be held until further investigations could take place. Desearo himself had not been seen or heard from since then.

Everything inside of the museum was carefully packaged and removed from the premises. It was then placed in a secure warehouse. And right now, it was supposedly undergoing a thorough investigation by the Tribunal in tandem with the Order of Guardians.

Jody had not given me an update on that in over forty-eight hours.

Hmm...

I needed to get my hands on that stuff. I needed to see what I could find out. I stopped walking around the room and ignored the murmurs of my father and Jody. They meant well, but I was still annoyed with the two of them.

Sunlight streamed in from the large picture window behind my dad's large leather chair. I followed a random ray of gold with my eyes fixed to a spot on my father's cluttered desk. I saw a legal document poking out from underneath the pile of folders that sat there. I spotted the word 'amulet' and my name, 'Angela Tanner'. Without thinking, I slowly exposed the paper and removed my cell from my pocket. Without noise or opening any apps, my cell took a photo of it. As if it knew what I wanted.

Hmm..

"So do we have a deal, Angela?"

"What? Um, sure Dad, you know what's best."

I kissed my Dad on the cheek as Jody shook hands with him.

Now. I had a plan.

———

"You did *what?!*"

I was not prepared for Jody's reaction to the snapshot I took of my dad's file. I mean, *chill out, dude.*

"Look, I didn't steal anything, Jody, I just took a picture of this paper! Besides *my* name is on it, so it's kind of my right!"

"Um, no, nope. Not how that works, Angela." Jody's exasperation was evident, but I couldn't understand why.

Didn't he want to help me?

"Look, if you don't want to come with me, then don't. I can call an uber!"

"As if I would let you go alone!"

"Alright, that's it! I don't care if you are a big bad Guardian, I am a Witch and I so do not need your help or permission, got it." I poked Jody in the chest with my purple painted fingernail. This may very well have been our first argument and my chest was heaving with anger.

Well, it *was*, until I saw Jody's chocolate brown eyes dip down to my figure and stay there a split second. When he raised them back up to mine, they were the color of dark, dark cocoa. Like those 90% cacao bars he was always bringing me.

His lips parted and I found mine doing the same. I had never felt anything like this before. Not with anyone else. His lean hands reached up gently and held both sides of my face. He moved in closer, leaning his entire body on mine. Jody's kisses weren't like anything else in the world.

He kissed me full on the mouth with everything that he was feeling. And boy did I feel it too. Whatever anger I was trying to hold on to dissipated in that instant. His minty cool breath met my own cinnamony warmth. The taste on my tongue was all sugar and spice and bubbles. An effervescent explosion of salty sweetness.

"Wow," Jody whispered, his forehead touching mine as we both worked to catch our breath.

"Yeah, ditto." I kissed him again, but this time he pulled away.

"Angela, uh, we have an audience."

I turned around to see Carol staring at us, open

mouthed, from the entrance of the TGE building. I put my hand over my mouth and felt more than saw my cheeks heat up.

"Uh, Carol?"

"Um, yes, Miss Angela your father asked me to catch you before you left. He wanted you to have this."

She held out her hand. In it was a small ivory envelope. I knew without looking what would be inside. The photograph of me and my mother. I couldn't stop the tear that fell from my eyes. I didn't even want to. I wasn't ashamed of it. I gave Carol a quick hug, delighted by her shocked response.

"Tell him thank you for me. And thank you, Carol, for bringing it down."

"You are most welcome, sweetie, and, um, I won't be telling your father what I saw when I caught up with you!"

She winked and I smiled back, embarrassed beyond belief. I watched her go inside then turned back to Jody.

"So tomorrow, okay?"

"Yes, tomorrow. But Angela, we need to stop by Sherry's place. Julianna is there."

7

KEEPING MAGIC

THE ANGELA TANNER FILES
VOLUME 2

I could hear Julianna's shrill voice from the street. I could only imagine what she must be thinking. I almost felt sympathy for her.

She must have skipped class to be at Sherry's this early. She was probably feeling pretty apprehensive at best, and at worst, well, my guess was she was there already.

"Alright, look, who are you, weirdos! And what happened to me the other day? And OMG! Are you kidding me, buddy? What the heck are you supposed to be? Get out of my way!"

"Sit down, little girl!" Vasco's voice betrayed his lack of patience. I rolled my eyes at his mocking tone. He wasn't exactly my biggest fan either.

Whatever.

I knocked on the door before opening it.

"Great! Who else is coming to this illegal freak show? Oh my God, Tanner? What is going on? Are you behind all this? Is this some kind of freak revenge? Am I being punked?"

"Julianna, just calm down, okay. Why are you here?"

"I don't know, okay. I went to school today and everything was fine until lunch. Then I got this feeling that, like, something of mine was missing. I searched the gym, my homeroom, and my locker, but I couldn't find anything. Then I just wound up here! In *Freak-show-ville*!"

"Okay, just calm down. The last time I asked if you remembered anything you got real upset, so maybe you could just tell me what you think you are missing?"

"Look, Angela, I know something weird is going on, okay, I just want this feeling to go away. I mean, I just can't deal with this now. I have a new routine for the cheerleaders designed specifically for the Zephyrs Basketball team and I, like, can't be seen here!"

I could not believe she was taking that kind of tone with me. I looked around, bewildered by everyone's mild reaction to this loud bossy little b-word! Sherry just sat there, quietly sipping her ever present mug of tea, while Vasco, Sherry's new BFF, paced the floor.

Everyone had stopped what they were doing in the middle of Julianna's little tirade. She was so ungrateful. Not to mention mildly insulting!

Enough of this nonsense.

"Are you serious? We saved your life, you vapid bit—"

"Thank you, Angela." The cool hand on my shoulder helped me rein in my temper. "Maybe you should go sit with Sherry for a minute." Jody's eyes laughed, but his voice was even.

I rolled my eyes and walked into the kitchen, but I was still within ear shot of them.

"Who are *you* supposed to be? A *Cullen* or something with all that black you're wearing? And I really hope that's faux leather, buddy!"

"Uh, what's a *Cullen*? Never mind. Miss DiPaolo, my name is Jody Nieves, I'm a Guardian. A sort of magic cop."

"A *what*?"

"Look, I get it. I understand you may not have the knowledge of your true background, but let's not play any games here. You've been a part of something. Something that has awoken the magic in your blood. It is my job to make sure that all supernatural forces are wielded within the laws of our kind. And part of that, is seeing to the safety of newly talented or magicked Witches."

"What are you talking about? I, I don't know anything." But the venom in her voice was gone. It was replaced by something else.

Fear.

The mighty cheerleader was frightened.

She held her arms tight around her flat stomach. Geez, she even made the mud brown gym uniform look good. Her baby blue eyes stared in disbelief at Jody as he said his next few words calmly. I admit I couldn't believe my ears either.

"You have Witch blood, Julianna DiPaolo. Your mother has neglected her duties in keeping this from you and she will receive a warning."

"My mother? This is her fault?"

"It is no one's fault. Magic simply is. Her neglect in informing you will be addressed. Now, the powers you unleashed yesterday have been bound for now, but that is not a permanent solution. Besides more of your magic may awaken."

"But I don't want to be a Witch! I just want to be normal! You've got to help me!"

"I am sorry, but it is not legal to take someone's powers away without cause. Give it time to sink in.

Now, should you wish to receive training you can call this number any time day or night. Okay?"

I couldn't believe it. He was giving her his phone number! Okay. I admit it. I was jealous. I could feel my fire itching under my skin. It wanted to be let out. I wanted to burn that piece of paper right out of her perfectly manicured little hand. But I didn't. I guess I had some control, after all.

"I told you guys that I remembered something about you, Angela, and Grazi. I get it now. I get it now! You're like a Witch or something. But she isn't. Grazi is *different*."

"Yes, she is. And she saved your life. Look, Julianna, I know you have all other stuff that is more important to you. But this, *Magic, Witches, us,* this all has to remain secret. Got it?"

"Oh, like duh! Like I'm gonna go post it all over the place or something! *Whatever*."

"Well, this has been an exciting day. Now, dear..." Sherry's voice was light and unaffected by the tension in the air as she directed her speech to Julianna, "You can go home now, but my doors are always open to you. Oh, one more thing, I meant to tell you this the other night, whoever it is that does your hair, well, they are using too much powdered bleach. That is why you must condition constantly. Now, if you come in here on Wednesday, I can have it done for you with a much better result. And I can also help you find and master your gifts."

"It is too much bleach! I told her that! Ugh. Um, okay I'm due for a touch up this week, but I'll come here instead?"

"Yes, that will be fine. Jody? Can you and Angela drive her home?"

"Um, sure. But I only have my bike?"

"No worries, you may take my car."

———

Sherry's vehicle of choice at the moment was a little yellow VW buggy. It had white leather seats and chrome plating. It was freaking awesome, but a bit cramped. Of course, Julianna insisted *she* sit in the front.

With Jody.

Grrr.

"So, Tanner?"

"What?" It was hard to talk since my right knee was digging into my stomach, but I managed it.

"That thing I'm missing. You have it then?"

"Uh, yeah."

"It's still nagging me, is there a way you can hang

onto it for a bit then give it back, like after March Madness?"

"Uh, I don't know. But I'll see what I can find out."

———

We dropped Julianna off at her house. It was bittersweet to pull into Grazi's driveway and not have her there. Nonna Rosa wouldn't be there either. For me, it was as if the entire heart of the place had been ripped out of it.

Julianna didn't seem to notice. I mean, the house looked good and all. That was something, at least. Julianna's dad was really keeping up with the grounds work. I think he was a landscaper or something. I didn't know what her mother did, I only knew she was a Witch with little to no powers. Hopefully she would guide Julianna in the way of light, and all would be well.

Hopefully.

Julianna got out of the little yellow car without even saying goodbye. Maybe she was having a harder time than her perfect face and clothing let on? I wouldn't spend too much time worrying about it. I had other things on my mind.

Anyway, we went back to *Shear Magic* and swapped Sherry's Bug for Jody's Ducati. Then we headed back to my house.

My father wasn't home yet. I could tell by the empty driveway. But this wasn't anything new. He worked very long hours. Always did. The only thing new was the sensation of a thousand butterflies flapping their wings inside of my stomach when I thought about being alone with Jody.

We entered my suite of rooms. I flipped on the light switch and tossed my jacket on the coat rack. Jody hung his up as well. I ducked my head and walked straight to my desk. I flipped open my laptop and keyed in my password. The information I learned from the memo from my father's desk was fresh in my mind. I wanted to research it immediately.

"Jody, what if Desearo is trafficking in more than stolen amulets and illegal supernatural artifacts?"

"What do you mean?"

"Well, that stuff we found in his museum was worth millions, some of it priceless even! But what if it is about more than the money? What if it is about the power? I mean, those relics held magical stores the likes of which our Coven hasn't seen in ages. And what about the others? What are those things worth to other Covens, Clans, and *whatever's*?"

"Yeah, I see your point, but—"

"I have so many questions! Who is gathering that much power for? Himself? Then why didn't he just drain them?"

"I think I know the answer to that, Angela. Desearo is smart. If this is about the power, then he knows that he needs a whole Coven of Witches behind him to move that much magic. One Witch alone would never survive such a huge transfer. He would need others to filter the power through to him. And ancestral magic does not like being transferred to someone outside of the family line. In fact, it can be fatal to the Witch who tries it without certain protections in place." Jody sat in the chair next to me.

He sounded worried. I clicked on my cell and scrolled to look at the picture of the document from my dad's office. There was an address on the top. I googled it and pulled up a map of the street and surrounding area.

It was not far from the museum itself. It was the warehouse, simply titled Warehouse #3. It was located in an industrial part of Morristown. The property was owned by the Coven Reallta, leased to the Tribunal, and used for evidence storage in supernatural investigations.

"We should go here tomorrow and see what we can find out."

"What is it that you think we are going to find out, Angela?"

"Well, we could see if anyone has tampered with any of that stuff. You're a Guardian, can't you see if there was an attempt to break open the magic?"

"Well, now that you mention it, there is a spell, more like a ritual, really, that I can perform to uncover past events. It would show us if anyone had tampered with the evidence."

"Sounds like that would be perfect."

"Okay, but, Angela, I don't like involving you. I'm going to talk to my superiors, and we will go investigate. I am guessing something like this will take a few days, but I'll check in with you whenever I can. Okay?"

"No way I am going in the middle of all this!"

"You need to go to school."

"But I can help! I can—"

"It's *my* job. And I don't want you anywhere near the Tribunal."

"Jody—"

"Angela, *please.*" He kissed me on the lips and any protests I would have made died. It was hard to think when he was kissing me. I suspected that was one of the reasons why he did it just then.

Better not be the only one.

"I'll call you. Goodnight, sweet."

Jody left and I found myself utterly exhausted. I showered and changed into a pair of lime green fleece pajamas with bananas all over the pants. The front read "I go bananas for you" in a bold yellow cursive font.

Goofy, but cute.

I plopped down on my light pink duvet. I had about a dozen pillows in all sorts of colors and prints scattered across my king-sized bed. I liked a lot of space when I slept.

It was one of those nights where even though you know all you want to do is sleep, your mind doesn't seem to get the picture. Jumbled confused thoughts just kept popping into my head.

Was Desearo working alone?

What was he after?

Did he kill my mother?

I didn't close my eyes until well after three o'clock in the morning. That was when I heard my Dad pull into the driveway. I didn't realize it before, but I think I was worried about him. After that, I slept like a baby.

The next day at school passed slowly. I walked

around as if I was in a daze. Junior year was a little rougher than I was used to, but I did okay.

I was almost jealous of the kids going on college tours and planning their spring break vacations. Normals didn't realize how easy it was for them. Compared to magic training, college prep seemed like a breeze.

Some Witches went to normal college. I mean, my dad did, though he went to a Witch run graduate program. Coven law was a force unto itself and took three years to master.

Most Witches chose to apprentice older members of their Coven in whatever field or environment they were talented in. Agricultural and/or artistic careers were the norm. Every now and then, we'd get a journalist or news anchor or businessman, but they were rare.

My dad was a businessman and a lawyer. Not exactly the dream child of his apple farming parents. But they had liked his orchard. I remember them helping with it when I was little. They used to visit during holidays until they passed away. They might not have understood, but they were always there to encourage him.

As for me, well, I was a techie with a knack for computer apps and online games. We were definitely a little strange as far as our Coven was concerned. Though, Dad did have a decidedly greener thumb than I did. Our orchards were awesome this year.

I understood the relationship between our healthy orchards and dad's healthy business all too well. He explained it to me thoroughly. Like every year when he made me help him distribute fertilizer amongst the rows of budding trees.

When I was ten, I asked him why we didn't hire a gardener and he explained that he could, indeed, hire a service, but then *he* would not be giving back to the Earth and the universe. And if *he* didn't give back, then *he* could not take. *Give and take.* It was an easy enough concept.

I was too worried about my whole Witchy powers being on the no-no list for the Tribunal and the inner evil workings of Desearo and missing Grazi and figuring out who I really was to worry too much about something as simple as college. I mean, *whatever.*

School, like NewsFlash, seemed too typical a path for me. I couldn't even focus on getting through the day. By eighth period, I was completely zoned out. I didn't even hear Mr. Connelly yelling my name until he was right in front of me.

"Ms. Tanner, do we have a problem here?"

"Huh? Um, no. No, sir."

"Yes, well, that is reassuring, but that was the bell, young lady, and I think you have somewhere else to be. I know I certainly do."

"Uh—" I couldn't wrap my head around what he was saying. All I could do was stare at the coffee stained spittle that flew out of his mouth as he yelled at me once again.

"Oh, are we happy to be procrastinating? Do we have nothing to do today? Look, I said get a move on, Tanner!"

———

*T*wo *days*.

And yet they felt like weeks.

Who knew that forty-eight hours could tick by so slowly?

I finished all of my homework for the week. I washed three loads of laundry, rearranged my drawers, cleaned the bathroom, stocked my little kitchenette with some healthy snack options and loads of water, and I even swept the floor. I was going nuts.

I twirled my hair into knots and even bit my nails down to stubs.

Oh well.

I supposed I could always get tips, but what was

the point really?

I'd just rip them off as well.

By the third day, I was a nervous wreck. I had to ask Sherry for a special meditative tea just to calm me down after school. It tasted like dirt.

Blech.

Finally, he came to my house that Friday evening. I was so happy when I heard the door that I wasn't even aware of his state for full on five seconds. I had never seen him like that before. His clothes were dirty and torn and he was sweating profusely. When he saw me, he almost fell down on the floor.

"Oh, *thank the Goddess*, you're here! You're safe! *Angela, sweet.*" He practically collapsed right there on my stairs. Relief flooded his features. I reached for his elbow and helped him inside. The smell of cold burn and ozone surrounded him. I knew what that meant.

Magic.

He had been battling *something*.

"Jody! What is it? What happened to you?"

"It's Desearo, and it's worse than we thought. Get Sherry and your dad."

"Okay, I will. Come in, sit down."

"Right, yeah, just a minute." I watched as he lifted his left hand, the one with the Pentacle on it.

I had yet to ask him about it. I mean, I am a Witch,

I know why the star is important to us, but why did he have it just there? My thoughts were interrupted the second he began casting. Jody's voice had a deep sing-song quality that made the hair on the back of my neck tingle. His casting reminded me of cool breezes and peppermint leaves.

He was a gifted Witch, that much was evident. Otherwise, the Guardians would never have chosen him for themselves. They were a secretive organization. But the supernatural world as a whole had come to rely on them to settle disputes and keep the various races in check for the last thousand years.

And that was about all I knew about them. Except that this particular Guardian happened to be someone I cared very much about.

Maybe even loved.

I didn't know if I was ready for all that. I was just seventeen and I had a few hiccups that might seriously dampen my social life in the near future. My newfound powers would more than likely be deemed illegal by my kind. I might be stripped of them, *or worse*.

Love was something I didn't have time to think about. Not just yet. I just liked being with him. It felt good. For now, that had to suffice. Jody's spell brought me back to the present:

"All ways West,

All ways East,

Change the path which led me here,

Those ill-wishers who follow,

Footsteps of mine,

Make them hollow,

Take them now,

Take them clear,

Take them far away from here,

Those won't find,

Those won't see,

As I will, so mote it be."

His hand glowed for a minute, then he really did collapse. Right on my floor. I grabbed my phone and called Sherry and my Dad. I didn't know exactly who hurt him, but they would pay.

I felt more than saw my eyes shift from hazel to a blazing red.

They would pay.

I'd make damn sure of it.

———

"Okay, Jody, repeat what you just said, more slowly."

"Really, Dad? He's gone over it enough times. We need to do something!"

"Angela—" But my father's voice was cut off by the only person in the room that I would listen to right then.

Jody.

"Angela, it's okay."

I sat down next to where he rested on the green velvet couch in my living room area. Sherry walked in from the bathroom and placed a white cloth, moist with water and healing oils, on Jody's forehead. The strong scent of lemons and rosemary entered my nostrils. It was supposed to have a soothing effect, but Jody cringed with pain when she put it in place.

"I am sorry for your pain, Jody. And, Angela, I know you must think I'm being unnecessary, but he needs to be perfectly clear about the events that took place."

"It's okay, really. So, when I left here the other day, I called Garren Hamza. He is a Guardian. He is a Chief Investigator in this territory. He has been responsible for my training since I was twelve years old. We went to the Warehouse together."

"That is where the Tribunal sent all of the magical artifacts seized from Desearo's museum?" Sherry blotted Jody's forehead once more. Then she moved her medicinal attentions to a long and angry red gash on his right forearm. I cringed as she tore his blood stained sleeve off his bruised and wounded flesh.

The monsters!

"Yes. They were supposed to be cataloguing the items and then they were to be sent to secure storage until their rightful owners could be found and notified on what to do to have the items returned to them. Only, when we got there, the Warehouse was empty. The security guards turned on us after we asked some questions. They were not humans, not Witches, they were—"

"Goblins!" Sherry exclaimed as she pulled a crooked black fingernail out of the gash on Jody's arm.

"Yes, Goblins! And they had a serious attitude problem. Garren followed their leader into a tunnel, I lost track of him. I had one against the wall in cuffs. He told me all about Desearo's real job. He *sells* magic, *stolen* magic. To anyone with enough money."

"That is an outrage!" Sherry was fuming she was so angry, but then again, I never knew anyone to revere magic quite the same way as my mentor.

"What was their role there? And, did he mention

any of Desearo's contacts?" My father was always practical, and these were surely good questions. I just had no patience for them right then.

"Hired thugs. Promised them some free potions and magic of their own. Too stupid to know Witch magic is no good to them. I asked after contacts, but he didn't know any. He did say there was someone helping him. High up. And he said Desearo wouldn't rest until he caught himself his biggest prize of all. Then two more Goblins came out of nowhere, big guys, they fought with spiked clubs and ancient Goblin spells. I almost didn't make it back here."

"What is this big prize he spoke of then, young *garda*? He steals priceless artifacts and family magic and sells them to the highest bidder! He has no soul! What more could the monster want?!" Sherry paced as she spoke, little sparks of magic seemed to fly off her of their own will.

"Yes. What does Desearo want from all this?"

The room seemed to grow smaller as Jody sat up. He looked at each person standing there until his dark, stormy eyes rested on my face. I wanted to know the same thing everyone else wanted to know.

What did Desearo want?

Then it hit me.

"A Fire Witch."

8

KEEPING MAGIC
THE ANGELA TANNER FILES
VOLUME 2

I couldn't believe I was at school. It took way too much energy to even pretend my class work mattered to me anymore. I couldn't even see the point of being there. I practically stomped my feet and demanded to stay home, but my father and Sherry both insisted I continue to behave as I normally would.

Until we had a plan.

We didn't want to tip our hand to Deseato should I be on his radar. I wasn't sure if he even knew that *I* was the Fire Witch.

All the uncertainty and the extra precautions were beginning to make me feel claustrophobic. Like there was a noose around my neck and it was slowing being tightened by some unseen goons.

What the heck?

I wanted my life back!

I walked through the hallway at school and ignored attempts by people I used to consider my friends to talk to me.

How could I even begin a conversation?

What would I say?

Hey girls! So, my weekend plans involve not being kidnapped by a traitorous Witch who wanted to steal my talents, keeping my magical powers a secret from the Tribunal, and helping my boyfriend recover from his latest life-threatening fight with a bunch of Goblins. And you? What are you guys doing?

Sounded perfect.

Ugh.

Jody was at my house right now. Well, at *my dad's side of the house.* He needed to rest after Sherry treated his injuries last night. Goblin scratches and bites were often poisonous. Since there were no actual tests until the injured was already dead, it was best to treat his wounds as if they were positive for poison. That meant a rigorous spell and antivenin potion.

The latter was foul smelling and thick as mud. Poor Jody had to drink an entire bowl of the stuff before Sherry even began to cast the purification spell. That caused Jody's body to writhe and shake with pain for a very long time. Afterward, he coughed and dry heaved for what seemed like hours.

It hurt me to see him in so much pain. I wanted to be strong for him, but I am afraid I cried out once or twice. And the tears, well, I couldn't stop them from falling, either, but I never left his side. Not until this morning when they made me go to school.

I just wanted to be home. To see his face. To know he was okay. I knew he was strong, but I felt uneasy being away from him.

Uneasy and angry.

Sure, I needed to know that Jody was going to be okay. And I wanted to be home more than anything. But I also wanted to find Desearo. I wanted this nightmare to end, once and for all.

The Coven Reallta was a small group of Witches compared to some Covens, but old families still existed among our ranks. And so did old justice.

Desearo didn't deserve a trial.

He was the lowest of the low. A scam artist. A confidence-man, unworthy of the name Witch. He ripped off anyone in the supernatural world who had anything of value. He was methodical and relentless, using long cons or downright theft to take magic that did not belong to him.

He was a traitor to our kind. A traitor to all magic.

And the Dark Witches and other supernaturals he sold his ill-gotten gains to, well, they were just as guilty. They needed to be caught and stopped.

Seeing Jody stumble in last night was frightening. Terrifying even. And so was the news he brought with him. All of the magical artifacts that had been seized from Desearo's museum had been stolen. Every single piece. By him of course. And probably with the help of someone in power.

My father texted me during my brief lunch. I didn't even feel like eating. And today was pizza day! I took my lunch period in the library. That only made me feel more alone. Grazi and I spent so much time in there. Putting away books and gossiping.

I missed her.

I had just sat down at our old table when he texted.

He confirmed what we already knew. The artifacts from the museum had not been reported missing. In fact, the cataloguing had been stopped for some reason earlier in the week. He also found out the Tribunal was not in the habit of employing Goblins at their Warehouses.

Not that they were prejudiced or anything, but Goblins tended to look at Witches as food rather than bosses. A bit of a PR nightmare, really.

If that was a scary thought, even scarier was the

fact that Goblins now worked for Desearo. A man with no respect for life, especially not our way of life. He must have promised them something big to have their loyalty.

Magic.

It had to be.

And what magic was he looking for now?

Mine.

He wanted my powers. A Fire Witch's powers. I wonder if he knew that Fire Witch he hunted was from a line hundreds if not thousands of years old.

I couldn't believe that I had only just discovered all this about myself.

Finally.

After months of tap dancing around the truth with my dad. Now that I knew, I found myself in more trouble than ever before.

I had no choice, but to share the truth of my ancestry with Sherry. Especially now that it seemed as if I was heir to more power than I had ever dreamed could be true. More power than I wanted, truth be told.

But what choice did I have in any of this?

Madame Magdelena hinted at this the other day. But now it hit home. I am a Fire Witch. With generations of magic at my fingertips. Many thought my kind were dangerous. Too dangerous to live freely in the supernatural world.

They claimed I had an uncontrollable hunger for power that wasn't mine. They wrote bedtime stories about the likes of me. To scare little Witches into behaving. As if I was some kind of monster.

Be good or the Fire Witch will come and steal your powers!

So far, none of that was true. Yes, I *heard* my powers after I took Julianna's magic from her and bound it inside of me. Yes, it craved more, wanted me to release it, but I didn't! I didn't give in to it!

So far, I've been able to control it. I haven't encountered anything I couldn't handle. And it seemed to me as if perhaps I was being judged a little prematurely.

I mean, seriously?

What's with all the hate?

Besides, the only one taking powers that weren't theirs was Desearo.

I should be home with Jody or out there trying to find where Desearo was hiding out.

I should not be here.

And yet there I was, next period. Pre-calculus. As if that was ever going to be useful in my life.

Ugh.

When the last bell of the day finally rang, I almost leapt out of my chair. I rushed down the hall to my locker and quickly opened it. Two minutes later, my worn penny loafers pounded the linoleum tiles until I exited the building to be greeted not by my boyfriend on his black Ducati, but by two huge men in a tinted Lincoln Town Car.

Whatever, I knew they would get me to him fast as they could and then I could formulate a plan. I recognized one of the drivers as a tall blonde with striking blue eyes I had had once before. I smiled and headed toward them.

He was wearing sunglasses, but I figured with the way the sunlight bounced off the snow that still covered much of the ground that made sense. He was one of the regular drivers from the chauffeur company my dad hired for me since I was old enough to go out by myself.

He was large too. Like, over six feet tall with big burly muscles. I guess I never realized that my drivers were also bodyguards. I shifted my backpack on my shoulder only to have Julianna step right in front of me.

Great.

What now?

"Hey, Angela." She looked around as if to make

sure we weren't seen. "I just wanted to say, you know, thanks and all. And, uh, tell Jody that I had that talk with my mom. I'm going to spend a few days with my grandmother, my mom's mom, she's got a place in upstate New York. I'm going there for spring break, anyway I wanted you to know..."

"Sure, Julianna."

"Oh crap, I'm sorry for this, really." She straightened her shoulders and gave a fake sort of laugh. "As if, Tanner! Whatever, like, I don't even know you for you to be talking to me."

"OMG, Julianna, what's with the geek squad?"

"Yeah, right! Like, hey, need-to-get-Tanner, you don't even go here!"

Her blue eyes pleaded with me to understand. I figured she had enough to deal with, so I just walked away with my head down. *As if* she could actually hurt my feelings.

The nasty comments and dirty looks didn't matter to me, not anymore. But surprisingly enough, they seemed to matter to her. She mouthed an *I'm sorry* as she tossed back her hair and caught up with her clones. I guess wonders never did cease.

I played along with my head down and even gave my shoulders a fake cry shake for good measure. At least, until I got into the car. The guy who was in the passenger seat got out and took my backpack and put it in the trunk. I smiled and said thanks as I continued with the façade that Julianna had embarrassed me yet again. Then, he closed the door and shut me inside.

I lowered my window as I passed Julianna and I met her eyes. She looked worried, but I winked and quickly rolled it back up. She smiled and continued to walk toward the gym with her clones.

I guess it wasn't easy being her either.

Huh.

Who knew?

Grazi said things like that all the time. I wondered what she would say if I told her her cousin was a Witch of sorts.

Ha.

That would be a great conversation!

LOL.

I really missed my friend. But I knew she was where she had to be.

I stretched my arms and rotated my head on my neck. I didn't realize I was so tense. I couldn't wait to get home. Take off my uniform. The yellow and brown polyester was a sick joke, if you asked me. It was worse than any other Catholic School uniform I had ever seen. For real.

The sky was as gray as the sidewalks as it flew by

my window. I wondered when the snow would finally melt. The temperature was almost sixty degrees. February in New Jersey was a very interesting month. It could be twenty degrees one day and sixty the next. And that was without magical interference.

It was just a few more days until Valentine's Day. I was so sick of the winter. I wondered if I would feel any closer to spring on the 14th?

Hmm...

I noticed the car speeding up as we neared the corner.

"Hey, you missed the turn! My house is that way."

"Your house, Miss?" My usual driver lowered his sunglasses and smirked at me in the rearview mirror.

My heart began to thud. Instead of blue eyes looking back at me, I saw orange ones with great oval pupils. His face seemed fuzzy, out of focus. It wasn't until I saw his green mottled skin peek through that I realized he must have used a glamour spell to disguise himself. This was so not the usual bodyguard my dad hired. This guy wasn't even human.

Goblin.

A Goblin was driving the car.

But how?

Goblins didn't have the kind of magic to pull off a glamour that lasted that long!

I tried the handles on both doors, but they were locked. I smacked and pushed them, but they did not budge. I tried to roll down the windows, but they were locked too.

"Now then, little girl, who said we were going to take you home? We thought we'd take you to lunch." The Goblin's voice grew less human with every word he uttered, until at the very last it was nothing more than a deep growl. A mockery of human speech.

"Maybe you will be our lunch, *Witch*," the other one joined in and snorted at what he probably thought was a clever addition to his friend's comments. He earned a smack on the back of his head for his troubles.

"Quiet, *Griefson*, you know our job!"

"*Hssss*. Ouch, *Angson*! You listen too much to the male-Witch. We are Goblin folk, we eats little Witches!"

"Not this one. Not now. Maybe we gets grubs *later*."

"Laters is better than nevers."

I shuddered as they grunted and growled ways to kill and eat me. Apparently, Witches were especially delicious slow roasted with cherry tomatoes and garlic.

Who knew?

I gulped and closed my eyes. This was not a joke. I almost liked my chances with Desearo better.

My phone!

If only I had my phone.

But it was locked in the trunk.

I whispered a prayer to both God and Goddess. Coming to peace with both of my religions was never easier than when I was in trouble. And I was in serious trouble here!

"And no Witchy powers, little Witchy! Look here, we've got the Iron Stone!"

He raised his green three clawed hand where he held a multi-colored stone. Its surface was smooth and round. It was almost the same size of the Goblin called Griefson's hand. The more I stared at it, the weaker I felt.

Iron Stone.

Hmmm.

That sounded vaguely familiar to me. I wondered if the Goblin was speaking the truth. I tried to remember one of my earlier lessons on Witchcraft. It was an old one from back when I was just a kid.

"There are three ways to stop a Witch's power, Angela, do you know what they are? One is a binding spell, this is a highly complex piece of magic that takes time and skill, but it is also the only way to ensure that the Witch's powers are, in fact, gone. Another way to stop a Witch, is to place protection seeds and herbs around

your home or office. And the final way, is to use special crystals or stones that are good at blocking magic or weakening one's powers. Of these stones, Tiger Iron is the most widely used. It has a broader range of protection. You see, it is the combination of three minerals, Hematite, Tiger's Eye, and Jasper. You can recognize it by the stripes of glittering black, gold, and red that swirl through and around the stone. It is quite beautiful, but when activated by someone with a talent for protection spells, it can make an enemy Witch feel lethargic and powerless. There are ways to block these things of course..."

Sherry's lilting voice echoed across my mind. I wondered if I concentrated enough if I could recall the rest of the lesson. I needed to counter the effects of the stone. If only I could just remember. I yawned and rubbed my eyes. This was so not good.

The car swerved in and out of traffic as we entered the Parkway. I hardly recognized a thing. I bit my lip and wondered how long it would be until they noticed something was wrong.

The two Goblins shed every last trace of their glamour. It must have been a weaker spell than I first thought. Their skin was varying shades of green, their heads bald, with pointed ears and long hooked noses. They had sharp teeth and large mouths with big, drooling lips. When they spoke now, it was in an incomprehensible language.

Worse was their smell. They burped and farted as if that too were part of their communication. With the windows rolled up I had to fight my overactive gag reflex to stop from puking right then and there. I was almost grateful that the stone made me weak. That was my last thought as I faded into unconsciousness.

9

KEEPING MAGIC

THE ANGELA TANNER FILES
VOLUME 2

"Where the heck am I?"

I opened my eyes to find myself bound with duct tape to a cold metal folding chair. I couldn't move. There was a large ceramic vase sitting on the floor in front of me.

Alone, it was rather ordinary. Something you might see in a hotel lobby. You know the kind, full of fake flowers or painted branches in the wintertime. It was about three feet high and emerald green in color.

There was a large cork topper on the floor beside it. So this was more *vessel* than *vase*.

Oh crap.

That wasn't good.

Large stones surrounded me in a wide circle. There were several that I recognized and many I didn't. *Tiger*

Iron, Moonstone, Bloodstone, Black Quartz. These were all used for protection against magic. Whoever was behind this was trying to keep my powers at bay.

I wanted to try to free myself before anyone came in, but it was difficult to move. And my thought process seemed slower than usual. I could not even think of casting. Not without my cell.

Besides, the words wouldn't come. My powers felt far away. It felt wrong in there. Tight and uncomfortable. I sucked in the dank air faster and faster. My chest started to feel small and constricted as I grew weaker.

"You must calm yourself. You are hyperventilating." I recognized Desearo's voice from the last time we met. Fear spiked through me.

He stepped out of the shadows and placed a hand on my cheek. His hair was no longer streaked with gray. He seemed thinner. And younger too. *Another youth spell*, I guessed.

He walked over to me in soft-soled leather shoes. They didn't make a sound on the damp concrete floor. He had refined tastes. I knew a little about men's fashion. Between his hand-tailored navy-blue suit, to his hundred-dollar pair of socks, this man liked to dress well.

There was one light in the room. A long plain wire hung form a metal rafter with a single bare bulb attached to it. It hovered directly over my head. The one hundred or so watts made seeing the rest of the dark room very difficult.

It threw me off balance, like it was supposed to do. I knew I was in some kind of abandoned building, but that was it. I had no idea where I was. Only that it smelled a little like vinegar.

The idea that I had been *kidnapped* from school sent my head reeling. I had no way to warn or contact Jody, my father, or Sherry. That made me panic even more.

I didn't have asthma, but I imagined it felt something like that. My eyes teared as I tried to get oxygen into my lungs. The air seemed too thick to breathe. Like sucking a milkshake through a coffee straw.

I couldn't even flinch away as Desearo got closer. All I could do was try to breathe. He placed his short fingered left hand on my face. I wanted to turn my head, but I couldn't as he held me there. His hand felt smooth, like plastic, fake and cold.

He rubbed my cheek in small circular motions as he breathed in and out slowly. I began to mimic him without realizing it. Soon, my chest didn't feel quite so tight. The room seemed a little less scary. And I was able to use my voice once again.

"Let. Me. Go." I didn't like the way my voice trembled, but I managed to look him in the eye as my anger rose with each spoken word.

"Yes, there it is. My, my, my. Look at that! Your eyes, they turn red when you are mad. Did you know that? The eyes always give you away. Every single time. Almost as much as that wild mane of red curls you wear on your head like a crown, little *Fire Witch*." He breathed the word right in my face and I think my heart stopped for a moment inside my chest.

He knew.

"What are you talking about?"

"Do not play coy with me, Angela Tanner. We both know you are the one. The first Fire Witch of your Coven in a hundred years. But I will tell you a secret. You are the second Fire Witch I have ever seen. And I am over three hundred years old!"

"Look, I don't know what you think you are going to get out of this, but—"

"Ha, ha, ha, my dear Angela, I am going to get it all. Every last drop of power. You see this circle? The stones that I have placed around you. They are working even now to keep your powers asleep. I have killed for these stones, Angela, that is how important you are to me."

"You're a thief and a murderer."

"Yes, well, small prices to pay for greatness. My

Goblin associates, Griefson and Angson, they have many more of their horde with them, and they will help me drain you. By the time I am finished, you will be gone, and I will have secured your powers in that jar."

"But you can't!"

"I can and I will."

"But why? Why are you doing this?"

"Why does anyone bother doing anything? Money and power."

"You have sold your soul for money and power?"

"My soul was bartered the day I was born."

"But what do you think you can do with my powers? They are too new, too raw—"

"I'll sell them to the highest bidder, after I take some for myself, of course." He snickered as he walked away.

I struggled against my bonds, but it was no use. I couldn't move. The back doors opened and at least twenty more Goblins entered the room. They varied in size, but one thing was certain. They were there to drain me. To steal my powers.

I was a failure. The powers my mother had died to give me were just now awakening and this man was going to take them from me. I trembled with grief at the thought.

"Angela, let me tell you a little something about your history. Would you like that? Thousands of years ago, you would have been worshipped, like a queen! Did you know that? No, I can see they did not tell you that. Ha! But I will not lie to you."

"All you do is lie."

Desearo did not like being interrupted. Anger and madness flashed in his eyes as he straightened his expensive tie and smoothed back his dark hair. I could tell he did not like being out of control. His zeal was almost uncontainable as he got more and more into his speech.

"No, I will tell you what you truly are. Where you come from. Fire Witches were revered for their powers and, of course, feared as well. They were believed to have been gifted by the Goddess herself! Favored among all Witches. They ruled the Covens, met out punishments, awarded the loyal, and, of course, they took what they wanted."

"That doesn't sound like anything I would want to be."

"Yes, power is uneasy for some. It is no easy thing to rule. They were secretive. Taking lovers to have heirs. Never revealing the child until the mantle had been passed. You see, a Fire Witch's lifespan was very long. And, of course, they never married as their craft was everything to them. The first Fire Witch to fall in love broke this rule. She married a man, beneath her, of course, a lowly Witch! A peasant compared to her! And she bore him a child, a son. Then she was betrayed by her own heart. Stupid fool!"

"How was she betrayed?"

"Her husband crept into their bedchamber with a silver athame carved with sacred runes and he slit her throat in the night thinking he had a direct line to her powers through their mutual son. He did not know that a Fire Witch's powers only passed to females of their bloodline. That secret is one I had only recently discovered. It is thought to be luck, or rather bad luck, of the draw. And so, for hundreds of years that particular line bore only male sons. Until such a time came that a daughter was born in the late 1690s. By then, the rumor of the evil Fire Witch had grown to such great tales of terror that this new Fire Witch was forced to keep her powers hidden. She kept her secret. Married a man she was told to by her father. And then one night, in the dead of the most cruel winter the New World had seen, she gave birth to a son. She used her powers in front of a trusted servant to create a fire, to warm them, to save them from certain death while her husband was away hunting. The servant, of course, told everyone she could about the occurrence. Because they were afraid, others in her Coven conspired against her. She was killed. Her throat cut as she suckled her newborn."

"How do you know all of this?"

"I can still taste her blood on my mouth every time I tell the story of how my mother was assassinated by my own father on the day I was born. Women, you see, have always been the creators of power and men the stealers of it. I am simply fulfilling my role as my father's son."

"Why? Why not defend her now?"

"Oh, I had my vengeance when I shot my father with an arrow through his icy heart. But now, I am a simpler man. I do not want revenge. No, I crave the powers I am denied because of my gender."

"But why not have a daughter? And teach her to use her powers for good? No one needs to be afraid of Fire Witches anymore!"

"Ha! Cruelest of all is the truth that *I* am unable to have children. In three hundred years, not once have I spawned a single child. So, this is the only way for me to get my hands on the power. And I shall have it. And I will sell it to the enemies of Witches everywhere. Traitorous Witches who murder their wives and set their children aside when they discover how weak they are!"

I swallowed the fist-sized lump that had formed in my throat.

He was insane.

Completely mental.

And I was the object of his delusions. I couldn't let him drain me.

But how would I get out of this?

No phone, no ability to cast, no Jody to rescue me. Ugh, great, I was a regular damsel in distress!

What would my Women's Rights teacher think if she saw me like this?

Desearo raised his short hands and the Goblins flanked me. He spoke to them in their own language, a series of growls and grunts. I had no idea what he was saying. But the combined stench of that many Goblins belching and flatulating was enough to make me sick.

One approached me with a sideways gait that reminded me of some kind of crab. In his three clawed hands, he held a bowl of dark and slimy looking liquid. He reached into it with one claw and pressed the stuff to my forehead. He drew across my head and down one side of my face with the muck. All part of this ritual to drain me, I guessed. I tried to squirm away, but another Goblin stepped forward and held my face firmly between his claws.

"We shall begin the chant!"

Desearo grabbed the empty green jar and sat it downright next to me. He held a book in his hands with ancient runes carved outside of it. He nodded his head and some of the larger Goblins stepped forward and bent down.

What were they doing?

It was still difficult for me to focus. I was so very drowsy and frightened. The combination left me too weak to even try and get a handle on my situation. Then suddenly, the fog around my head started to lift.

Those big Goblins that Desearo had called forward were moving the magicked stones. Desearo started chanting loudly in a language that I didn't understand but guessed was some sort of bastardization of Latin. The smaller Goblins began to cast in their own unintelligible speech.

A searing pain started in my body as they grew louder. I felt a burning sensation, like the worst pins and needles in the world, underneath my skin. It was my magic. It was writhing and churning as something was trying to rip it from my very being.

As the fog began to lift more and more, the pain began to come on stronger and stronger. It was my guess that Desearo needed to move the stones completely in order for him to successfully cast his draining spell. And he needed the Goblin's magic to try and focus my powers into the jar.

"Furtum ignis, facies ejus, conportabis hic, furari flamma, facies mia..."

His Latin sounded crude, but maybe that was because the spell was old. I wasn't really in a position to criticize; I just wanted the pain to stop. I needed help. I had to have faith in my father, in Sherry, and most of all, in Jody. They would find me. I needed to believe that, but in the meantime, I had to hold on.

"From the East, North and West,

Though it's dark night,

Bring forth the day,

Bright as robin's crest,

In this way, make them pay."

A blinding light to match the sun's sent the Goblins ducking for cover. Desearo screamed at them to stop. But it was too late, the light was still blinding them, and they were running for cover. All Goblins had a serious allergy to sunlight.

"Come on, Jody!" I whispered to myself as exhaustion crept over me. That small cast was enough to drain me of the scant amount of energy I had managed to conserve since this ordeal began. I closed my eyes on the horror of Desearo gathering the scattered Goblins back in line.

My plan failed.

———

"Have you seen Angela?"

Julianna's head whipped around at the sound of Sherry Morgan's voice addressed to her in front of her entire cheerleading squad in the gymnasium at Sacred Heart Prep.

"Um, excuse me, but you can't, like, be in here." Lizette gave scathing look at the eccentric dress that Sherry was wearing and rolled her eyes.

"Can't I? You know, you really shouldn't use so much foundation on such young skin. It will prematurely age you." Sherry's eyes glowed for a second, though she carefully looked down. Lizette grabbed her compact and shrieked at what she saw. Age lines and spots on her seventeen-year-old face!

"Oh my God!" The other cheerleaders ran with her to the bathroom, but Julianna stayed behind.

"That was mean," Julianna said with a smile. "But she's kind of a bitch, anyway. Okay, so yeah, I saw Angela after school. She got into a black car with a couple of goons."

"Tell me everything."

―――――

"She's been what?"

"Angela has been kidnapped. You did not send a car for her, Frank?"

"No, I mean, *yes*, I did send a car, but they just called to tell me their driver was found tied up in a gas station bathroom not far from the school." Francis Tanner threw his phone on the counter in disgust.

"Dammit!"

"Wait, I have an idea, did you say you saw Julianna?"

"Yes, Jody, she's probably still in the gymnasium." Sherry looked curiously at the young Guardian. The hell he had been put through the last twenty-four hours would have sent lesser men to their graves. But this one had heart.

"Send Vasco to get her, now."

―――――

Ten-minutes later, the door to the Tanner home flew open and Vasco entered with Julianna in tow. She had a piece of duct tape over her mouth and she was furiously trying to rip it off.

"Vasco," Sherry scolded and snapped her fingers. The tape dissipated as if it was nothing more than dust.

"I apologize, Julianna, but we need your help."

"Well, you guys have a funny way of asking for help!"

"Angela was kidnapped by those men you saw today. Now, she stepped up and helped you when you needed it. Will you help her?" Jody's voice pleaded with her. She took one look at him and nodded her head.

"Okay. What do you need me to do?"

KEEPING MAGIC

"Do not remove the last stone yet. She stirs." Desearo halted his chant as he stepped toward me. He lifted my face by my chin and gave it a shake.

"One more step in this ritual, little one, and you are Fire Witch no more." He smirked at me as he lifted a dagger. I flinched and tried to move away, but I was too weak. My magic was being siphoned and there was nothing I could do.

"Did I mention you won't survive this? Ah well, too late, can't leave this unfinished now, can I?"

I sat up in my binds. Desearo raised the dagger. He was going to bring it down right into my heart! I was going to die. At seventeen. Tied up and bound by a madman who wanted to sell my powers to the highest bidder.

I didn't want to die. There was so much I wanted to live for. But I was powerless. Just as the last stone was lifted by the biggest Goblin there, his hand moved and in that same instant the back doors of the room blew open.

Jody, Sherry, Vasco, another Witch I didn't know, and my Dad came running through it. It was the best damn thing I ever saw. They used swords, spells, and fists against the onslaught of Goblins.

"No!" Desearo screamed and moved toward me, his hand outstretched. He started chanting again, but a lightning bolt of black feathers came shooting in and the book was ripped from his hands.

Vasco.

"You will pay for that smile." Desearo backhanded me and I saw stars. But it was worth it.

The force of his slap turned my head almost all the way around. Without it I would have never noticed that the last protection stone had been moved. The circle was broken.

I closed my eyes and focused on my powers. Those that were left inside of me and what was stolen in the jar to my right. It felt like eons passed before my power came rushing back into me with all the force of a tsunami. When I opened my eyes, Desearo was trying to escape. And I realized everything I saw was red.

I surveyed the room. The five Goblins surrounding my father went up in smoke with one thought, the same happened to the ones who were hitting Jody and whoever that was with him with Goblin spiked clubs.

Within seconds of me regaining my powers all of our enemies fell. The rest of the Goblins were captured in a circle of flames. They were placed in magicked handcuffs.

Then there was Desearo. I found him in a fetal position on the floor. He had crawled back to the jar, but, of course, now it was empty.

"Oh Goddess, you are everything I thought you would be! I apologize, great fire mother. Yes, cleanse your son, set fire to my body!"

The fog of power was almost greater than the fog that had clouded my mind when he was draining me. But hearing Hector Desearo call me 'mommy' was enough to snap me the heck out of it!

I shook my head and the flames that encased my body were instantly put out. I couldn't say the same for my clothing, but thank the Goddess for Sherry and her long ivory poncho.

I put that on and watched as the Witch, the one I didn't know, put magicked handcuffs made of black iron on Desearo. He seemed to pull them from thin air. The same spell Jody cast to store his helmets.

Hmm.

Then I learned his name. This was Garren Hamza. He was Jody's boss.

———

"Okay, the Guardians are taking Desearo into custody. Now, the Tribunal is demanding he be handed over to them, but we're delaying the transfer."

"How will you do that? Jody? You won't get into trouble, will you?"

"Who me?" His beautiful smile caught me off guard, almost as much as the quick kiss he dropped on my mouth.

I turned my head, a smile on my face, to see Vasco looking at me. His frown was great, and his forehead creased with worry. Sherry spoke to him, but he shook his head and in a flurry of movement, took off as the same raven that saved me earlier.

I wondered if I should maybe send him a gift basket to say thanks.

Chocolate.

Chocolate was always a hit.

Then maybe he'd get off my back?

"Do not worry about him, dear." Sherry's lightly accented voice was like music to my ears. I ran into her arms as she held them for me.

"Thank you so much, but how did you find me?"

"Not me, dear, your young man. He had the idea to use the little Hound's cousin to find you."

"Julianna?"

"Indeed. He told us of how you had not absorbed her powers. Then he asked if maybe we could use the ones inside of her to locate you, since they are inside of you as well. And it worked!"

"Thank the Goddess!"

"Indeed, child. Now, how are you feeling?"

"I felt good, like all charged up. You know what I mean?"

"Yes, well, sometimes the rush of power gets us going, yes?"

"Yes, but Sherry, the others. They are all steering clear of me."

"*Hmm.* Perhaps it is to give you space? You are wearing only a poncho, after all."

I thought about what she said, and it was possible my father and the others were steering clear of me because I was barely dressed. I hoped that was the reason. And not because of what I was afraid of.

They were scared of me.

———

I found Jody in the kitchen in my dad's house after I had showered and dressed. He must have too, because his dark hair was wet, and he wore a pair of too big gray sweatpants and a white t-shirt. I've never seen him in anything other than his usual black garb. He looked great.

"Jody?"

"Hey, did you want a sandwich?"

"Um, sure." We got out all the fixings to make a couple of turkey sandwiches. It seemed so wonderfully normal to be doing this simple thing together. I almost didn't want to talk about anything else.

"Sherry told me what you did to find me."

"You mean get Julianna over here?"

"Yeah. That was really smart."

"I just thought, what would Angela do?"

"Really?" I was flattered that he thought I was so smart. And courageous. He risked a lot for me. His life. And now he was risking his neck as Guardian. I felt guilty.

"Did I, uh, freak you out too, when I did my Witchy stuff?" I had to know the truth. The others would need time to adjust. Jody was the first one who found out what I was. But he had never seen me do anything like that before. I mean, those Goblins that I destroyed were literally erased off the planet. Like, not even ashes were left. I needed to know if he was afraid of me too.

"Are you kidding me? You are freaking awesome! And the only Witch I want next to me when the bad guys are raining down on us." I ducked my head and laughed a little at his tone. He sounded like a kid reading a comic book.

But what had happened was no comic book. This was real life and he had risked his, again, to save me.

Would the guilt ever go away?

"I didn't mean for this to happen. For you and Garren to have to defy the Tribunal. For you to get hurt," the last part was whispered, and I could hardly look at him. But he wasn't having any of that. He turned me to face him and spoke so gently my heart melted.

"That part is our job. And you are in no way responsible for it. Hector Desearo is a criminal, no doubt, but he is a stooge. He has a boss, and we are going to find him. The Tribunal needs to be vetted. It is a tough job, but it has to be done. And having you safe is the most important thing in the world to me, okay?"

"I am sorry. I feel like I made you do this, like it's my fault—"

"Angela, that is ridiculous. And even if it was true, I'd do anything for you."

"Jody—"

"I'd walk over hot coals for you. I love you, Angela." He looked into my eyes and I saw the truth in his.

My Guardian.

I reached over and placed my hand inside of his larger one. Then, I squeezed. Tears spilled from my eyes as he gathered me in his arms and our lips met in a soul-shattering kiss. A kiss to send all others flying out of my mind.

He loved me.

"There is just one thing I need to know."

"What's that?"

"Will you be my Valentine, Angela Tanner?"

"Yes, definitely, yes," I whispered the last yes as our lips met again.

I had my powers, I knew the truth about my mother, and I finally had a Valentine of my very own.

I was the luckiest girl in the world.

The End.

Thank you for reading The Angela Tanner Files, I sure hope you enjoyed them. These books were written simultaneously to the Grazi Kelly Novels and if you try them out, you are sure to see Angela within the pages.

You can grab more books from the Grazi Kelly Universe today, starting with Wolf Moon by clicking here.

Thank you and happy reading!

LOOK FOR MORE YA/URBAN FANTASY FROM C.D. GORRI

Welcome to my Young Adult Urban Fantasy Books!

Including:
The Grazi Kelly Novel Series
The Angela Tanner Files
G'Witches Magical Mysteries Series

& New Adult Urban Fantasy
The Witches of Westwood Academy
Blackthorn Academy for Supernaturals

To me, the world of the paranormal is full of endless possibilities. As a writer, I can take advantage of that. I can introduce old ideas through new characters and situations. And hopefully, I can entertain you while trying to do just that.

All of my books are set in the same paranormal world and mainly take place in my home state of New Jersey. I call it the Grazi Kelly Universe in honor of my first heroine, Maria Graziana Kelly aka Grazi (grah-tzee). Characters and creatures overlap, but each series can be read alone.

So far, I've expanded this world to encompass Werewolves or Wolf Shifters, Witches, Demons, Dragon Shifters, Bear Shifters, Fox Shifters, Jaguar Shifters, and more! It is my intention to continue to build this world with every book I write.

Del mare alla stella,
C.D. Gorri

EXCERPT FROM HUNTER MOON

Chapter 1

Tearing through the bitter cold in the dead of night should have been scary. The frigid air made streaming clouds of my breath as I ran through the woods. An enormous black Wolf to the left of me pulled his mouth back, revealing long sharp canines. He howled and plunged ahead. A few inches to his right and he could have easily taken me down. Of that I have no doubt. I wasn't afraid though. I was exhilarated.

The full moon shone down through the trees. It threw shadows off the tall pines, birches and oaks. We ran for about fifteen or twenty miles. It was difficult for me to tell as I hurried to keep up with the rest of the pack. The scenery sped wildly by, but I was much too aware of everything not to notice. I flew past towering walnut trees and bare forsythias. My large forepaws pounded the earth as I launched myself over fallen branches and dried out shrubs.

The smell of the woods mixed with that of my companions filled my sensitive nostrils. I could make out each distinct member of our party by scent alone. I listened and was deafened by the beating of our hearts, our breathing, the scurrying of small forest animals avoiding us, and the hoot of an owl as it clung to a tall tree overhead. *Overwhelming?* Maybe at another time I would have felt that way. But this was different.

It wasn't exactly as if time had slowed down. It was more like I was *in* every moment. Something I had never experienced before. I had no idea where we were going. I blindly followed the pack. Too focused on everything and everyone around me to be worried about something as ordinary as our destination.

My gaze landed on Ronan. He was ahead of me by a body length. I could make out every single strand of his red and gold fur. It made his coat glow like fire when the moonlight hit it. He moved on four legs with the same beautiful grace that he did on two. I often found myself watching him at school or when we jogged together. He was fast and agile. But more than that. He was *elegant* for someone so tall and muscular.

I wondered if I moved like that too. Was I graceful and competent? I didn't used to be. But everything was different now. He turned his long lupine head toward me. His green eyes burning in the darkness. I snorted at him and he yipped. He was checking on me as he had done several times. I didn't resent it as much as I pretended too.

It was the first time I'd run as a Wolf in the company of others. In fact I'd never seen a pack before. Even a small pack as this one was. I had googled Wolves in my spare time and knew I was much larger than a wild grey Wolf. Seeing the others before me made me realize I was, if anything, average sized for my kind. My fur was a dark brownish color and I had a platinum streak running down my muzzle. It matched the one in my hair that I got after my first change. I'm almost used to it. Well, at least I don't jump every time I see my reflection anymore.

I already knew what my Wolf looked like. I've seen her in my mind's eye, when she spoke to me. I knew the form I took now from my pointed ears right down to the tip of my furry tail. I was stronger, faster, and a lot more lethal like this. I think I might even weigh more as a Wolf than I do as a girl. My appetite certainly has increased. I'm thinking it must have more to do with my Wolf side since I haven't gained all that much weight. The pounds I've put on seem to be mostly muscle anyway. I am totally good with that since I looked a little like a string bean before.

The full moon hung low in the sky. Huge and golden it touched me with its light. I felt whole and strong with power. The air was thick with it. I used to always think of darkness when I thought of the night. But not now. *The true light of the moon and the stars is always present, but we can only see it in the darkest night.* That's something my Uncle Sean told me. He was right. It was incredible. Especially through these eyes.

Uncle Sean's huge shaggy blonde Wolf ran directly behind his father, Rolf. He was larger than the all of the rest of us except for my grandfather. He was a massive white Wolf with steel gray eyes and an unmistakable air of dominance. He led the hunt. Uncle Sean had advised me before we changed that this is the way it was done. Werewolves are pretty serious about their pecking order. Alpha's tended to get snooty if anyone ran in front of them. It was in their nature to be first, to guard the pack from whatever may lie ahead.

I ran somewhere near the back of our party. I wondered what that meant for me in the greater scheme of things. Guess I'm pretty low on the dominance list. That's just fine with me. The other Werewolves spent a few minutes snapping and growling before order was established and Rolf commanded we move. Ronan stayed near me and kept tabs throughout our run. There were four large Werewolves that flanked us on all sides. One was the black Wolf who liked to show off his fangs, two more were gray and another was a honey color. Guards, all of them. I didn't know their names. They hadn't been introduced to me when we met at my grandfather's new home base, which incidentally happened to be next door to my house.

Maybe I should back up a step. My name is Maria Graziana Kelly, most people call me Grazi (*grah-tzee*). A few months ago, I found out that I'm a real live Werewolf. Yup, that's right, I tend to get furry around the full moon. I'm also bound by an ancient pact my ancestors made to serve with the Hounds of God. They're like this mega Wolf pack who technically work for the Catholic Church. The Hounds have been fighting an age old battle against covens of Witches who want to claim dominion over the Earth for the Devil. You heard me correctly, I seriously mean the actual *Devil*.

My father before me was a Hound. He and my mother died fighting this battle when I was about three years old. I keep a picture of them next to my bed. I was raised by my maternal grandmother, Nonna Rosa.

Hard to believe? *You betcha.* I didn't really buy it either until last night when I got all furry and fangy and ripped the throat out of my high school librarian.

Of course, I only did that after she turned out to be possessed by a Wendigo. A ravenous Demon who was responsible for several local deaths including a student at my high school, Sacred Heart Prep. Wendigos eat their victims. They crave human flesh. The more they consume, the deeper the craving. Scary, right? But they aren't the only things out there. This world is new to me, but I have to survive it. *I just have to.* To find out what really happened to my parents. And to avenge them.

The eight of us came to a clearing in the woods. Ronan stayed by my side and I waited as Rolf continued in the lead. I had no problem keeping to the rear. It was his right to lead. He was, after all, the Alpha. He stealthily crouched down. Everyone stopped and mimicked him. I did too. I could smell the small creatures we were stalking and my mouth filled with saliva. *Ew.*

Ronan had told me before we changed that we were going hunting. *Rabbits.* Six of them were tucked into a hole beneath the cold, dried up grass. I could hear their tiny hearts racing and it made me salivate more. *Yuck.* I'd never eaten rabbit, but the beast in me could have devoured the lot whole. I shuddered. *I am so not normal.* I shook my head which earned me a stern look from Mr. I-like-to-show-off-my fangs.

Rolf signaled with a swish of his tail for the guards to come in closer. Another swish, the lowering of his ears, and the hunt began. Rabbits darted in all directions, sensing our presence, and we chased them. I watched Uncle Sean shake his prize in his jaws until the tiny creature's neck snapped. He was busy digging in when I felt something strange. I let the small brown bunny I was stalking go and picked my head up. It was like something was watching me. Stalking *me*, the hunter. I didn't like it.

While the other Wolves took advantage of the power bestowed on us by the full moon, I watched the woods.

Our four guards were no longer *guarding* us. They were caught up in the thrill and satisfaction of the hunt. Ronan, Uncle Sean, and Rolf seemed intent on the game also. *Not Me.* No, I felt *exposed*. Threatened. Something was definitely not right.

I scanned the tree line for something, anything that could explain what I was feeling. Rolf yipped at me. I made a move to join him, but stopped mid-step. Were-Wolves can communicate, but it wasn't like the way I had talked to Ronan before. It was more like images and impressions. I could tell he was not pleased by my behavior.

I felt Rolf trying to pressure me. To bend me to his will. *Hunt. Eat. Obey.* I wanted too, I really did, but I forced myself to step back. Away from him and his commands. Not without struggle, mind you. But I managed it.

He bared his fangs, flattened his ears, and loosed a short growl. *No.* I would not challenge him. I dropped my eyes and took another backwards step. He turned his back on me then. His attention back on his prey. A large brown rabbit. *Yum.* My Wolf wanted some of the succulent, juicy meat, but *I* was in control.

I sniffed the air. I smelled Wolf, rabbit blood, the cold forest, and something else. Something a little off. Waves of color surrounded the Wolves. Mostly the same reds, oranges. They were stronger around Rolf and Sean. My Wolf eyes watched the colors for a moment.

I didn't know what they meant. I looked at the trees and they too had their own colors, greens and golds. It was strange and beautiful. Another advantage of my Wolf's eyes perhaps? I could only assume so.

I walked slowly in a circle surrounding the others. The feeling was back. Someone or something was out there. I continued to look among the bare branches and frost covered bark of the surrounding trees. My body stopped moving the second I saw them. A pair of glowing eyes. The same set I thought I had imagined just last night from my bedroom window.

They held mine for a moment before disappearing. I took off at full speed heading for what, I did not know. Only Ronan seemed to notice. He yipped and followed me. I could feel his disapproval. He wanted to stay and enjoy his prize. His Wolf belly grumbled loudly. Hungry again, for sure. I loosed a short howl and charged ahead confident he'd follow. I was glad to have him. I mean even after everything I had seen, who knew what waited for me in the darkness?

I stopped short in a small clearing. Ronan skidded to a stop directly behind me.

Someone's here, Ronan.

What? Where?

Wait, is that you? Can you hear me like this too? It was like an open line of communication between my mind and Ronan's had opened up. His thoughts voiced clearly in my mind and his impressions too. The foremost one was his desire to protect me. Always.

Yeah, Maria, I think I can. This is crazy. We should get back to the others.

Why? They won't listen. Rolf won't listen.

Where are we going then?

I sniffed the air. I smelled forest, the cold, a faint whiff of a bear that must have passed within the last day or so, and Ronan, his Wolf musk pleasant to my sensitive nose. There was something else. It was mineral like. Iron or copper. Nope. I knew what it was.

Do you smell that, Ronan? It's blood.

Yes, I smell it. Let's get back. Rolf is angry and he's calling us, can you not feel him?

I can, but it's faint. I can shake it off.

What do you mean shake it off? It's deafening.

No, it's more like a whisper now that we aren't near him.

What are you, Maria Graziana?

I don't understand.

I know you don't. Let's go. We will report what we have found...

EXCERPT FROM G'WITCHES

The three Fairchild Witch triplets, Olivia, Esme and Agatha were huddled together in Aggie's room, sitting on her giant four poster bed and all staring at the crystal orb commanding their rapt attention.

"I SWORE I would never do this again," Esme said in a slightly peeved tone, "You remember what happened LAST time, don't you?"

"HUSH!" Olivia commanded, staring at the prismatic light dancing in the center of the crystal that appeared to be growing larger, "Aggie was in charge last time! This time I am! No mess ups, I promise!"

"Not to mention that Morphic Corporeal Magic is the hardest discipline in Spell Casting," Aggie reminded her mildly, refusing to take offense, "With the possible exception of Global Volcanic Eruptions and Pandemics! I just let the prism get too big before I started casting! And we got you back to normal in no time!'

"ANY TIME when you are sitting there with two boobs so HUGE you'd need a wheelbarrow to carry them in is too much time entirely!" Esme fussed.

"Well, now we know better," Olivia said in a soothing voice, "And so we will DO better."

"Who wants to go first?"

Esme sighed, "I will! But I'm NOT going for the full Dolly Parton or even Porn Star-I just want a D cup. Nice and round if you please, like hot air balloons!"

"You got it!" Olivia told her. Whipping out her wand she spoke a short incantation as she pointed the tip toward the prism captured in the crystal.

Esme gave a startled sound as the front of her tank top seemed to fill out instantaneously.

"OH, I FLOVE THEM!" she shrieked, grabbing a newly enhanced breast in each hand, "But do you think they're too much?"

" You mean will they attract attention? The WRONG kind, from the opposite sex?...Oh Gee I HOPE so!" Olivia said, giggling, "I mean isn't that the POINT?"

"Okay now me, ME!" Aggie said.

Olivia's lovely face took on a look of rapt attention as she again focused on the revolving prism captured within the crystal orb.

"LOVELY PRISM ARTISROUCHE
GRANT MY SISTER HER FLESHLY WISH"

Aggie gasped involuntarily as her breasts exploded into DD cups and the bra she was wearing ripped asunder in the middle. When the material in the blouse she was wearing made a stretching sound she quickly flung it off over her head and gazed down stupefied at her new bosoms.

Olivia was horrified, and waited for Aggie, who was frozen motionless staring at her new acquisitions with eyes like saucers, to start screaming.

Instead she began giggling, covering her breasts with her arms as she went off into gales of laughter.

"OH MY GOD LOOK AT THESE!" she said," WOW! JUST WHAT I WANTED ! I always wondered what it would be like to have hooters like these! Thanks Sissy, I FLOVE them!"

Olivia looked over at Esme , who also had a look of surprise on her face.

"Is THAT what you really wanted?" she questioned Agatha, "I mean they are VERY noticeable! If Witchcraft doesn't work out for you, you can always try to break into the adult entertainment industry! But...are you sure you didn't want them a teensy bit, *er*, less outstanding?"

"No they are perfect!" Aggie said, jumping up, "Only none of my bras will fit, and I'll be reduced to wearing only my stretchiest sweaters in the meantime. What do you think the boys will do? Do you think Harlon Piercewick will notice ?"

Olivia found herself a bit envious. Before all the breast augmentation spell casting she had had at least a double cup size on her sisters.

Now she looked, well, certainly not flat chested by any means, but smaller than the other two. Nevertheless she resisted a temptation to move her own *tatas* up another cup size.

Out of all three triplets, she was the most patient, composed and sensible one. Magic was glorious (and she was good at it), but could also be seductive and addictive, and SOMEONE had to keep her wits about her!

"Well, they certainly make a statement. I almost want to get you nipple tassels for Christmas so that you can practice that stripper twirling thing!"

All three of them erupted in laughter envisioning Aggie giving a show with her new hooters . Agatha was a performance person, loved to show off her magic and perform in plays at school, she certainly had the personality for it.

"OH, damn and shazam, we'll be late for class!" Esme said, glancing over at the clock, " Grab your short capes ladies! And Aggie, you can wear my cape from last year , I think it's the only one that will cover your new assets, you don't want to cause a horny schoolboy stampede do you?"

Even though Melvin, Audra's little brother was 18 months younger, he was in ADVANCED SPELL-WEAVING PLACEMENT(ASP for short), and so, his short cape sported a special embroidered ASP insignia with a snake.

He shared two of the same classes with his sister and the Fairchild twins. And there was a brand new teacher for the COMMUTATIONEM CLASS, a VERY tall Sorcerer that had recently arrived on campus by the name of Dr. Tantalus Banks.

Most of the girls in the class had developed an instant crush on him during orientation. He looked to be in his mid-thirties. Just old enough to have the older man allure, and in fact a lot of them referred to him as "tantalizing Tantalus", a name that quickly caught on due to his broodingly dark looks.

He dressed in black leather most of the time, with silver studded boots, straight dark razor cut hair, and curiously almond shaped green eyes that seemed to flash to a golden color when he became annoyed in class. All in all, his appearance was that of a heavy metal Rock God. Even the boy students thought he was cool.

The students soon learned that if they did not immediately cease talking by the time the school bell announcing the start of class ended, raindrops would begin to descend upon them even though they were inside the classroom. It would be a slight, faltering patter of rain at first, but after a minute or two would open up to a deluge if they didn't immediately pipe down.

Olivia thought Dr. Banks very clever, because it only took a few drops before the entire class had been shushed, largely through peer pressure from students that didn't care to get soaked, which was most of them.

The Barlow brothers wouldn't have minded of course, they were natural pranksters and thought most out of the ordinary things immensely entertaining.

"Attention class, I am Dr. Tantalus Banks, and I will be your instructor for Commutationem Class. I expect perfect conduct from each and every one of you AND your complete attention as there will be periodic pop quizzes administered here, by ME, to test your grasp of the arcane and powerful knowledge that will be imparted to you here. Now, do any of you happen to know the essence of what we will be studying here?"

It was no surprise to Audra or the Fairchild triplets when Melvin's hand shot up. He was a whiz at Latin and could actually converse in it.

"*Commutationem* is the term for 'exchange' in Latin," he said when Dr. T nodded at him, "And it is a magic of unknown origin."

"Correct," Dr. T said as he paced slowly at the front of the classroom, "Or more accurately, of origins so ancient that the threads of its beginnings cannot be traced. It is, however, regarded as a very useful Magic under certain circumstances...

...And what circumstances might those be? Does anyone in this class know?"

Aggie, Olivia and Esme, and a nice but shy student by the unfortunate name of Dicky Peters all raised their hands, but the Professor nodded behind them at Audra.

"Only under EXTREME circumstances," she began . But Dr, T cut her off by saying "Correct!" and pointing to Olivia, who still had her hand held halfway up.

"Define "extreme", would you Olivia," he said.

Olivia was amazed that he seemed to know her name already. She had no idea that their names were floating above their heads in glowing cursive letters and could only be seen by the teacher due to a spell he'd cast upon the classroom.

"Well, EXTREME meaning that it is a kind of magic that is not included in Freespell Magic, which is what Witches rely on most of the time. Commutationem Magic requires that some kind of exchange take place. In the common vernacular it is sometimes referred to as 'Barter Magic'."

"YES! And this is very important to remember. Although Commutationem Magic is virtually immune to warding or being blocked, it is not free, it will extract something from the Witch that uses it. Sometimes something as little as an eyelash or an inch of height-"

There was a rustling in the classroom as several of the shorter boys, including Dicky Peters, squirmed at the idea of losing any of their vertical growth.

"Sometimes it will grant the Caster its power, and then sicken them, or in extreme cases, even take a Witch's life.

It is tricky and unpredictable. Some call it "the magic of last resort", but I can teach you how to use it with caution if you should ever find yourself in a situation where normal magic is unavailable or ineffective..."

"We have always been warned not to enter the Conundrum Caverns," a young witch who wore her hair in two short braids that seemed to point in opposite directions murmured. As the Professor shot a look of slight disapproval in her direction her hand shot up, "Sorry Professor! I didn't mean to speak out of turn, but even though the caves are right behind the Whispering Falls, we swim in the pools below the falls when it's warm enough, we were told not to go behind the falls into the caverns because magic doesn't work there. Is that what you mean?"

"Yes, that would be one example Tracina, though I must remind you to refrain from speaking out of turn.

And there are many others. But through your studies in this class I can acquaint you with certain Spells that will minimize your sacrifice if you should be in a situation where you absolutely MUST use a "barter" spell. Just remember the creed that is associated with the Commutationem spell serves as a warning not to take advantage of its powers too lightly...

'TO WHOM MUCH IS GIVEN, MUCH IS REQUIRED.'

Now, while I have your attention I would like to

introduce to you my Teaching Assistant for this class. His name is Lapis Hart, and he is himself a graduate of the MAGNIFICO FINISHING SCHOOL for Magical Arts. He comes highly recommended, and I expect that you will grant him the respect he deserves."

"Where did HE come from?" Aggie murmured to Esme as a lanky yet handsome youth with long sun streaked chestnut brown hair over his collar appeared to step out from behind Professor Tantalus Banks and stand before them, looking around at the large classroom full of students and nodding . The Fairchild triplets were immediately struck by the fact that, though he appeared to be only a few years older than the students, he had a large lock of pure white hair in the front that gave him an unusual appearance.

"He's HOT," Aggie whispered to Esme. They weren't the only ones whispering after the Teaching Assistant made his appearance and as the whispers quickly grew in such volume, Dr. T rapped on his podium to restore order to the class.

The ancient looking leather bound textbooks were passed off by the Assistant Teacher from the wheeled cart and handed one at a time to the student at the end of each row to be passed on. The Assistant seemed pleasant enough, very friendly, though somewhat shy...

...ALTHOUGH, Olivia thought to herself, if SHE had to be Dr. T's assistant she would probably be afraid to utter a peep herself. She already felt sorry for him since Dr. Tantalus Banks had a forceful personality and seemed rather a bully.

"Well, THAT was certainly intense," Agatha remarked as the sisters left the classroom to breathe the less stuffy air of the high arched hallways, "That Teacher's Assistant to Dr. T seems very nice. And very adorable. I wonder how old he could be-he doesn't look very old!"

"I have no idea but look at all the boys staring at your latest acquisitions," Esme said as they passed male students walking in the opposite direction that seemed to be swivel-necking to take a second look at Aggie as she walked by, "I swear, it's got to be an instinctual thing. How Neanderthal!"

"Well, I expect it has everything to do with mating in the caveman era," Olivia said matter-of-factly, "I mean I guess big boobs and curvaceous hips meant women were good breeders!"

"And as far as the males went I suppose it was muscles and giant cocks," Esme said, "Well, that makes sense. I think I'm a little jealous, I think I wish I'd gone just a bit bigger with mine. How long until we can redo the spell Olivia? I know there's a waiting period or something!'

Olivia giggled.

"Just a 30 day one. Otherwise it can go haywire my greedy darling, and we don't want THAT again!

OTHER TITLES BY C.D. GORRI

Other Titles by C.D. Gorri

G'Witches 2: The Harpy Harbinger

G'Witches 3: Summoning Secrets

*****The following section is for mature readers as romance novels may contain adult content.*****

Paranormal Romance Books:

Macconwood Pack Novel Series:

Charley's Christmas Wolf: A Macconwood Pack Novel 1

Cat's Howl: A Macconwood Pack Novel 2

Code Wolf: A Macconwood Pack Novel 3

The Witch and The Werewolf: A Macconwood Pack Novel 4

To Claim a Wolf: A Macconwood Pack Novel 5

Conall's Mate: A Macconwood Pack Novel 6

Her Solstice Wolf: A Macconwood Pack Novel 7

Werewolf Fever: A Macconwood Pack Novel 8

Also available in 2 boxed sets:

The Macconwood Pack Volume 1

The Macconwood Pack Volume 2

Macconwood Pack Tales Series:

Wolf Bride: The Story of Ailis and Eoghan A Macconwood Pack Tale 1

Summer Bite: A Macconwood Pack Tale 2

His Winter Mate: A Macconwood Pack Tale 3

Snow Angel: A Macconwood Pack Tale 4

Charley's Baby Surprise: A Macconwood Pack Tale 5

Home for the Howlidays: A Macconwood Pack Tale 6

A Silver Wedding: A Macconwood Pack Tale 7

Mine Furever: A Macconwood Pack Tale 8

A Furry Little Christmas: A Macconwood Pack Tale 9

Also available in two boxed sets:

The Macconwood Pack Tales Volume 1

Shifters Furever: The Macconwood Pack Tales Volume 2

The Falk Clan Tales:

The Dragon's Valentine: A Falk Clan Novel 1

The Dragon's Christmas Gift: A Falk Clan Novel 2

The Dragon's Heart: A Falk Clan Novel 3

The Dragon's Secret: A Falk Clan Novel 4

The Dragon's Treasure: A Falk Clan Novel 5

The Dragon's Surprise: A Falk Clan Novel 6

The Dragon's Dream: A Falk Clan Novel 7

Dragon Mates: The Falk Clan Series Boxed Set Books 1-4

The Bear Claw Tales:

Bearly Breathing: A Bear Claw Tale 1

Bearly There: A Bear Claw Tale 2

Bearly Tamed: A Bear Claw Tale 3

Bearly Mated: A Bear Claw Tale 4

Also available in a boxed set:

The Complete Bear Claw Tales (Books 1-4)

<u>The Barvale Clan Tales:</u>

Polar Opposites: The Barvale Clan Tales 1

Polar Outbreak: The Barvale Clan Tales 2

Polar Compound: A Barvale Clan Tale 3

Polar Curve: A Barvale Clan Tale 4

Also available in a boxed set:

The Barvale Clan Tales (Books 1-4)

<u>Barvale Holiday Tales:</u>

A Bear For Christmas

Hers To Bear

Thank You Beary Much

Bearing Gifts

Also available in a boxed set:

The Barvale Holiday Tales (Books 1-3)

<u>Purely Paranormal Romance Books:</u>

Marked by the Devil: Purely Paranormal Romance Books

Mated to the Dragon King: Purely Paranormal Romance Books

Claimed by the Demon: Purely Paranormal Romance Books

Christmas with a Devil, a Dragon King, & a Demon: Purely Paranormal Romance Books

Vampire Lover: Purely Paranormal Romance Books

Grizzly Lover: Purely Paranormal Romance Books

Christmas With Her Chupacabra: Purely Paranormal Romance Books

Purely Paranormal Romance Books Anthology

<u>The Wardens of Terra:</u>

Bound by Air: The Wardens of Terra Book 1

Star Kissed: A Wardens of Terra Short

Waterlocked: The Wardens of Terra Book 2

Moon Kissed: A Wardens of Terra Short

*Now in a boxed set and in audio!

<u>The Maverick Pride Tales:</u>

Purrfectly Mated

Purrfectly Kissed

Purrfectly Trapped

Purrfectly Caught

Purrfectly Naughty

Purrfectly Bound

<u>Dire Wolf Mates:</u>

Shake That Sass

Breaking Sass

Pinch of Sass

Kickin' Sass

<u>Wyvern Protection Unit:</u>

Gift Wrapped Protector: WPU 1

<u>Standalones:</u>

The Enforcer

Blood Song: A Sanguinem Council Book

Spring Fling (co-written with P. Mattern)

<u>EveL Worlds:</u>

Chinchilla and the Devil: A FUCN'A Book

Sammi and the Jersey Bull: A FUCN'A Book

Mouse and the Ball: A FUCN'A Book

<u>The Guardians of Chaos:</u>

Wolf Shield: Guardians of Chaos Book1

Dragon Shield: Guardians of Chaos Book 2

Stallion Shield: Guardians of Chaos Book 3

Panther Shield: Guardians of Chaos 4

Witch Shield: Guardians of Chaos 5

<u>Howl's Romance</u>

Mated to the Werewolf Next Door: A Howl's Romance

The Tiger King's Christmas Bride

Claiming His Virgin Mate: Howls Romance

<u>Twice Mated Tales</u>

Doubly Claimed

Doubly Bound

Doubly Tied

<u>Hearts of Stone Series</u>

Shifter Mountain: Hearts of Stone 1

Shifter City: Hearts of Stone 2

Shifter Village: Hearts of Stone 3

<u>Accidentally Undead Series</u>

Fangs For Nothin'

<u>Moongate Island Tales</u>

Moongate Island Mate

Moongate Island Christmas Claim

<u>Mated in Hope Falls</u>

Mated by Moonlight

<u>Speed Dating with the Denizens of the Underworld</u>

Ash: Speed Dating with the Denizens of Underworld

Arachne: Speed Dating with the Denizens of Underworld

<u>Hungry Fur Love</u>

Hungry Like Her Wolf: Magic and Mayhem Universe

Hungry For Her Bear: Magic and Mayhem Universe

<u>Shifters Unleashed Boxed Sets</u>

Check out these amazing anthologies where you can find some of my books and the works of other awesome authors!

Midnight Magic Anthology (Water Witch)

Rituals & Runes Anthology (Air Witch)

<u>Island Stripe Pride</u>

Tiger Claimed

Tiger Denied

<u>NYC Shifter Tales</u>

Cuff Linked

Sealed Fate

<u>A Howlin' Good Fairytale Retelling</u>

Sweet As Candy (as seen in Once Upon An Ever After)

<u>Coming Soon:</u>

Asterion

Vampire Shield: Guardians of Chaos 6

Tiger Rejected

For Fangs Sake

Hungry As Her Python: Magic and Mayhem Universe

If The Shoe Fits: A Howlin' Good Fairytale Retelling

Chickee and the Paparazzi: FUCN'A

The Wolf's Winter Wish: A Macconwood Pack Tale

The Hybrid Assassin

Tempted By Her Protector: WPU 2

Alien Protector: WPU 3

Elvish Protector: WPU 4

Thrilled By Her Protector: WPU 5

ABOUT THE AUTHOR

C.D. Gorri is a USA Today Bestselling author of steamy paranormal romance and urban fantasy. She is the creator of the Grazi Kelly Universe.

Join her mailing list here: https://www.cdgorri.com/newsletter

An avid reader with a profound love for books and literature, when she is not writing or taking care of her family, she can usually be found with a book or tablet in hand. C.D. lives in her home state of New Jersey where many of her characters or stories are based. Her tales are fast paced yet detailed with satisfying conclusions.

If you enjoy powerful heroines and loyal heroes who face relatable problems in supernatural settings, journey into the Grazi Kelly Universe today. You will find sassy, curvy heroines and sexy, love-driven heroes who find their HEAs between the pages. Werewolves, Bears, Dragons, Tigers, Witches, Romani, Lynxes, Foxes, Thunderbirds, Vampires, and many more Shifters and supernatural creatures dwell within her worlds. The most important thing is every mate in this universe is fated, loyal, and true lovers always get their happily ever afters.

Want to know how it all began? Enter the Grazi Kelly Universe with Wolf Moon: A Grazi Kelly Novel or pick up Charley's Christmas Wolf and dive into the Macconwood Pack Novel Series today.

For a complete list of C.D. Gorri's books visit her website here:

https://www.cdgorri.com/complete-book-list/

Thank you and happy reading!

del mare alla stella,
   C.D. Gorri

Follow C.D. Gorri here:
   http://www.cdgorri.com

www.ingramcontent.com/pod-product-compliance
Lightning Source LLC
Chambersburg PA
CBHW071211210726
48293CB00002B/377